WARPED GALAXIES

TOMB OF THE
NECRON

WARPED GALAXIES

Book 1 ATTACK OF THE NECRON

Book 2 CLAWS OF THE GENESTEALER

Book 3 SECRETS OF THE TAU

Book 4 WAR OF THE ORKS

Book 5 PLAGUE OF THE NURGLINGS

Book 6 TOMB OF THE NECRON

Book 1 CITY OF LIFESTONE

Book 2 LAIR OF THE SKAVEN

Book 3 FOREST OF THE ANCIENTS

Book 4 FLIGHT OF THE KHARADRON

Book 5 FORTRESS OF GHOSTS

Book 6 BATTLE FOR THE SOULSPRING

WARPED GALAXIES

TOMB OF THE NECRON

CAVAN SCOTT

WARHAMMER ADVENTURES

First published in Great Britain in 2021 by
Warhammer Publishing,
Willow Road,
Nottingham, NG7 2WS, UK.

Represented by: Games Workshop Limited - Irish branch,
Unit 3, Lower Liffey Street, Dublin 1,
D01 K199, Ireland.

10 9 8 7 6 5 4 3 2 1

Produced by Games Workshop in Nottingham.
Cover illustration by Cole Marchetti.
Internal illustrations by Dan Boultwood & Cole Marchetti.

Tomb of the Necron © Copyright Games Workshop Limited 2021. Tomb of the Necron, GW, Games Workshop, Warhammer Adventures, Space Marine, 40K, Warhammer, Warhammer 40,000, the 'Aquila' Double-headed Eagle logo, Warhammer Age of Sigmar, Stormcast Eternals and all associated logos, illustrations, images, names, creatures, races, vehicles, locations, weapons, characters, and the distinctive likenesses thereof, are either ® or TM, and/or © Games Workshop Limited, variably registered around the world.
All Rights Reserved.

A CIP record for this book is available from the British Library.

ISBN 13: 978 1 78999 068 3

No part of this publication may be reproduced, stored in a retrieval system, or transmitted in any form or by any means, electronic, mechanical, photocopying, recording or otherwise, without the prior permission of the publishers.

This is a work of fiction. All the characters and events portrayed in this book are fictional, and any resemblance to real people or incidents is purely coincidental.

See Warhammer Adventures on the internet at

warhammeradventures.com

Find out more about Games Workshop and the worlds of
Warhammer 40,000 and Warhammer Age of Sigmar at

games-workshop.com

Printed and bound by CPI Group (UK) Ltd, Croydon, CR0 4YY

For George.

Contents

Tomb of the Necron   7

Galactic Compendium   205

The Imperium of the Far Future

Life in the 41st millennium is hard. Ruled by the Emperor of Mankind from his Golden Throne on Terra, humans have spread across the galaxy, inhabiting millions of planets. They have achieved so much, from space travel to robotics, and yet billions live in fear. The universe seems a dangerous place, teeming with alien horrors and dark powers. But it is also a place bristling with adventure and wonder, where battles are won and heroes are forged.

CHAPTER ONE

The Psyker

'What do you want?' the old woman snarled.

Zelia Lor wanted one thing and one alone – to get back to the ship. It wasn't enough that, together with her friends, she'd spent the last few weeks being hunted by some of the most terrifying alien races in the galaxy, now she was standing alongside Mekki and Talen in a stinking hovel, facing a wart-covered crone who wouldn't know dental hygiene if it bit her.

Grooda Vanikir was craggy-faced and snaggle-toothed, and smelled worse than a grox-paddock. Her home was a shack built in a waste pipe beneath a towering hive. A waste pipe that smelled only slightly worse than Grooda herself.

Captain Harleen Amity stepped forward, extending a hand in greeting, only to retract it seconds later when Grooda snarled like a rabid chemdog.

'I hear that you have certain… abilities,' the rogue trader said.

Grooda's bloodshot eyes narrowed. 'What if I do?'

Amity produced a bulging purse, which jangled as she waved it in front of the woman. 'Then you'll end the day considerably richer than you started it.'

Grooda shot out a bony hand to grab the proffered bounty, only for the rogue trader to snatch the purse away.

'You'll be paid after you've told us what we want to know.'

Hissing like a phyrr-cat, Grooda turned her gaunt face to Zelia and her friends.

'Are they yours?' she rasped, jabbing a

bony finger at the children.

The rogue trader's expression didn't flinch. 'I'm helping them find something.'

The old woman sniffed. 'What?'

'Pastoria.'

'Never heard of it.'

'It is a planet,' Mekki offered helpfully. 'Also known as "the Emperor's Seat".'

Amity shot the Martian a sharp look. She hadn't been happy about the children tagging along while she visited Grooda's lair.

'Why not?' Talen had asked.

'Because Grooda Vanikir is an unsanctioned, and often unpredictable, psyker,' Amity told him.

Talen's response had been characteristically overconfident. 'Then you'll need us to watch your back,' he said with a shrug.

Now, Zelia wondered if leaving the relative safety of their ship had been a mistake. The trek to the psyker's hovel had been long, not to mention disgusting. Rhal Screena was the capital city of a particularly downtrodden hive world. Its passages were dank and the crowds suffocating, too many sweaty bodies crammed into too tight a space. Even protected by Grunt, Amity's lumbering servitor, Zelia had felt ill at ease – unlike Talen, who had been in his element.

The former ganger had grown up in a hive – albeit one in much better condition than this – but Zelia had spent most of her life on archaeological digs with her mother. She was happiest in wide, open spaces, not at the bottom of thousands of tonnes of metal and rockcrete. Even after all this time, she found it hard to breathe in a hive, knowing that she could walk for kilometres and still not see the sky. But Amity had insisted that if anyone could find Pastoria – the legendary planet the *Zealot's Heart* had spent the last few weeks searching for – it was Grooda.

The skeletal woman peered at Mekki in the same way a spine-snake might scrutinise a tasty rodent. 'You're a Martian.'

'I am,' Mekki replied, his voice as calm and emotionless as ever.

'A long way from home.' Grooda's eyes crawled over Zelia and her friends. 'You all are.'

'You don't know anything about us,' Talen said.

'Don't I?' Grooda took in a shuddering breath and her eyes rolled up in their sockets. 'A planet torn apart by metal faces,' she rasped, her voice taking on a sing-song quality. 'Grinning faces. *Evil* faces.'

Zelia shuddered, picturing the monsters Grooda described. 'The Necrons. They destroyed Targian.'

Grooda's eyes rolled back down to fix on her, a pinprick of light seeming to glow behind pupils like black holes. 'And yet you survived. Little things like you.'

'We've done a lot of things,' Talen said, his tone hardening.

Amity stepped between him and Grooda before the former ganger could lose his temper. 'I see that the stories about you are true. You are a gifted woman.'

'Some would call me cursed,' Grooda rasped, nodding at the purse that was still in Amity's hand. 'But what you ask will cost more than a few coins.'

Now it was Amity's turn to narrow her gaze. 'How much more?'

Grooda glanced up at Grunt. 'A woman like me needs protection, especially down here in the pipes.'

Amity shook her head. 'I'm afraid that Grunt isn't for sale.'

'But I'm so weak,' Grooda continued, hunching over as she spoke. 'So vulnerable.'

Amity chinked the purse. 'Then this could buy you a weapon.' She cast a look around the ramshackle hut, from the rags that served as a bed to the crooked shelves smothered in spiderwebs. 'Or even the means to move somewhere more...'

Sanitary? Zelia thought to herself, although Amity finished with a simple: 'Secure.'

Grooda chuckled, the laugh descending into a gargling cough. 'I'll tell you how to find your planet, but it'll cost you.' Her rheumy eyes settled on the children once again. 'It'll cost them.'

Something moved behind Grunt. Zelia spun around. 'What was that?'

Grooda shrugged. 'Just one of my little pets.'

A shadow moved beyond the ragged curtain Grooda used as a door. 'It doesn't look that little to me.'

And whatever it was, it obviously wasn't alone. The sound of scurrying legs filled the pipe. *Lots* of legs, accompanied by the *clack-clack-clack* of snapping jaws. Zelia knew what was making the noise before they scuttled into the shack.

Long ago, when her father had still

been alive, Zelia had become entangled in a temple-weaver's web during the excavation of an old tomb on Araza IV. Her dad had got her out before the ten-legged monstrosity could attack, but ever since then she had been terrified of spiders. That's why no one could blame her when she screamed out in terror as half a dozen arachnids scuttled into Grooda's hut.

They were huge, each the size of a cyber-mastiff, their thick legs ending in wicked claws. Their swollen bodies were covered in coarse red hair, while their swaying heads were smothered in bulbous eyes the colour of pus-filled blisters. They surged forward, herding Grooda's visitors together, and even Grunt had the sense to avoid their snapping mandibles.

Grooda, meanwhile, was tickling one of the fearful things as if it was a faithful dog, even as the creature hissed and quaked, desperate to attack. Something was holding them back. Zelia

didn't know what, until she noticed that Grooda's eyes had become the same colour as the spiders'. Was she controlling them?

'Perhaps now you're ready to listen to my terms,' the psyker wheezed. 'To strike a deal.'

Amity slipped the coins back into her pocket. 'What do you want?'

Grooda released her spider and it scuttled forward to join its kin. 'I am old.'

'No kidding!' Talen snapped, never

taking his eyes from the twitching arachnids.

The psyker ignored him. 'Rhal Screena is not a place for the old. You will make me young again.'

Amity raised an incredulous eyebrow. 'How are we supposed to do that?'

Grooda jabbed a skeletal finger at the children. 'By giving me one of them.'

'One of *us?*' Talen parroted. 'Why?'

Amity's expression had turned grave. 'So she can steal your youth.'

'That's not possible.' Talen looked from the captain to the psyker, and then back at the captain again. 'I mean, it's not, is it? She can't really do that.'

'I have done it before,' Grooda cackled, 'and I will do it again.' She scraped a gnarled hand across her bald head, and flakes of dried skin dusted her thin shoulders. 'How do you think I've remained this beautiful for so many years?'

Amity took a step forward, ignoring the spiders who reared up to block her path. 'And you will tell us where to find Pastoria?'

Grooda nodded. 'I think that is a fair price.'

'I don't!' Talen said.

'Then take me,' Amity said. 'Take my youth and tell us what we need to know.'

Grooda chuckled, amused by the offer. 'You? You are old.'

Amity tried her best not to look insulted. 'I'm in my prime. Besides, I look better than you.' She offered the old woman a tight smile. 'No offence.'

'None taken,' Grooda said, licking her chapped lips with a black tongue. 'Very well. I shall feast on what years you have left.'

'No!' Zelia stepped forward despite her fear. The spiders hissed furiously.

Grooda tilted her head, her pack of arachnids mirroring the gesture. 'You have something to say, girl?'

'Take me instead,' Zelia said, the words spilling out of her mouth before she could change her mind. 'I'm the one who wants to go to Pastoria, and I have more years to give. If you want youth, take mine, just let my friends go.'

'You don't have to do this,' Amity told her, but Zelia stood her ground.

'Yes I do. We need you to pilot the ship.'

'I can pilot the ship,' Talen insisted.

Amity snorted. 'Thank you very much!' she said bitterly.

'You know what I mean,' he said. 'I just... I don't want Zelia to get hurt.'

'I'll try not to take it personally,' Amity muttered.

'The girl is right,' Grooda cut in, weighing Zelia up like a slab of meat. 'She is young... strong. She will do nicely.'

'What do I have to do?' Zelia asked, sweat trickling down her back.

Grooda's leathery face split into a hideous smile. 'Nothing too difficult. You just have to die!'

CHAPTER TWO

Battle of the Ages

'I... I can't move,' Zelia gasped as her arms and legs went rigid and she fell back to the filthy floor. It felt as if a great weight was pressing against her chest, each breath more difficult than the last.

She was vaguely aware of Talen calling her name, but couldn't hear above the buzzing in her ears. Her friends were at her side, their hands gripping her arms, trying to help her up. Even the lightest touch hurt, as if bruises were blossoming beneath their fingers. Everything ached. Zelia looked down and tried to yell out as she saw her hands. They were ageing before her eyes, liver spots blossoming across paper-thin skin.

Her cry was little more than a croak.

She forced herself to focus, telling Talen she was okay... even though it was obviously a lie.

'You promised us information,' she heard Amity snarl, even as Talen tried to pull her up. It was typical of the rogue trader. Business first. *Good.* Don't waste the opportunity. Don't waste the sacrifice.

In front of them, Grooda was laughing, her crooked spine straightening with a series of cracks and pops.

'And you shall receive it,' the woman replied, her voice noticeably stronger than before. She was getting younger by the second, even as Zelia felt herself withering like an old leaf. 'Show me a star map.'

'Should I?' Mekki asked, glancing worriedly at Zelia. She nodded, the effort sending pain shooting down her neck. She felt so tired, like all she wanted to do was sleep.

The Martian hit his wrist-screen, and a holo-map burst from his projector-bead. Constellations and planets flickered into life, their glowing light illuminating the gloom of the hut.

'Not so bright!' Grooda snapped, shielding her eyes as the spiders scuttled back from the display. Mekki complied, the hololiths dimming instantly, and Grooda went to work. Even as her skin smoothed, the now nimble psyker danced between the gently glowing stars, tracing a line through the galaxy.

'Here?' she asked herself, her now pupilless eyes scanning the map, before she changed direction, swinging her hand around in an arc. 'No, no. There it is. The echo of the Golden One. Yes, the path is clear. The path is true!'

'You know where we must go?' Amity asked.

'Pastoria awaits. And with it, your heart's desire.'

'Then give us the coordinates,' the rogue trader snapped. 'Zelia can't take much more of this.'

'I'm fine,' Zelia wheezed, although she obviously wasn't. She could barely lift her head. Talen was cradling her in his arms.

'Here,' Grooda said, a soft down of dark hair now covering her once bald head.

She was pointing at a portion of the

map that was largely devoid of stars, save for one solitary sun.

'Are you sure?' Amity asked.

Grooda beamed. 'As sure as my back is straight and my future is bright.'

'Then stop the... the ritual,' the rogue trader demanded, struggling to find the right word.

The psyker giggled playfully. 'Didn't you hear what I said? The girl knew the terms, as did you. She must die. *All* her years shall be mine.'

Amity's cutlass sang as it was pulled from its scabbard. 'Not on your life.'

'No – on hers!' Grooda exclaimed as the spiders surged forwards. Amity swung her weapon, only to have the cutlass knocked from her grasp by a ball of sticky silk. All of the spiders were spitting webs, which thudded against the captain's uniform.

'Grunt!' she barked at the servitor as she tried to pull the webbing from her sword hand. 'Do something!'

Grunt lumbered forward, his

hammer-like fists held high, but the spiders struck again, smothering the servitor in webbing. He let out a muffled howl and yanked at the thick silk that covered his eyes. Soon his large hands were gummed tight to his face.

'You shouldn't have provoked me, captain,' Grooda laughed, her skin flushed with stolen youth. 'Now the price has gone up. I shall have *all* your lives.'

Her eyes glowed brighter and Zelia heard Talen gasp. Wincing with arthritic pain, she turned her head to see Talen ageing before her eyes, his blond hair turning grey.

'Close your eyes,' Mekki spluttered. 'All of you.'

'Why?' Talen croaked.

'Just do it, Talen Stormweaver!'

Zelia was too weak to argue. She squeezed her tired eyes shut, just before a sudden light flared all around. Grooda wailed, her cry accompanied by a dozen high-pitched squeals from the spiders.

'Run!' cried Mekki.

Run? She could barely walk.

'I'll help,' Talen said, his joints cracking as he hauled her to her feet and lurched out of the hovel, Mekki and Amity right behind them.

'What did you do?' she whispered to Mekki as they stumbled down the pipe.

Mekki's voice was deeper as he replied. 'I noticed that the psyker was sensitive to light, probably after years of living beneath the surface – a theory that was proved correct when she reacted so badly to the glare of the map...'

'So you turned up the glow of the hololiths,' Amity croaked. 'Clever.'

Zelia could imagine the satisfied smile on Mekki's lips as he replied. 'I gambled that her familiars would share the same affliction, no matter how young their mistress had become.'

'You? Gambled?' Talen said, flashing a

smile. 'Who would have thought it?'

Mekki cocked a non-existent eyebrow. 'Certainly not me. You are a bad influence, Talen Stormweaver.'

'Whatever he did, it looks like they've got over the shock,' Amity said as the spiders scuttled after them.

'Can you climb?' Talen asked as they reached a ladder that led out of the pipe.

'I'll have to,' Zelia replied, although her arms proved too weak. She barely made it up two rungs before she slipped. She was caught by Grunt, who had ripped his hands free of his face, leaving painful red splotches around his eyes. Grooda's ritual – if that's what it was – seemed to have had little lasting effect on the servitor as he carried Zelia up the rickety ladder, the others following close behind.

The spiders were scuttling up after them by the time Amity cleared the hatch. Talen and Mekki shoved at the heavy lid, and its rusty hinge squeaked as it clanged into place, trapping Grooda and her spiders in the pipe.

'Do you think that will stop me?' the psyker screamed through the door, the hatch rattling as her spiders tried to push it open again.

'No,' Zelia said, snatching one of Amity's beamers and aiming at the lid, 'but this will.' She fired, melting the lock shut, leaving Grooda screaming in fury. The sound echoed in Zelia's head as the world spun around her. She didn't even hear the beamer clatter to the floor as she collapsed, and everything went dark.

CHAPTER THREE

After-Effects

'Zelia?'

Talen sounded like he was underwater, his voice distant and muffled. She tried to open her eyes, but they seemed to be glued shut. That was fine. She didn't want to wake up anyway. All she wanted to do was sleep.

'I think she's coming round!'

No, I'm not, she thought angrily. *Just let me be.* But sounds were swimming into focus all around her. Talen's voice. The thrum of void-engines. Boots against deck-plates.

'Let me get to her.'

It was Mekki's voice this time,

accompanied by a sharp pressure against her skin and a sharp hiss. She gasped in pain, sitting up only to cough uncontrollably.

'Try to relax, Zelia Lor.'

Try to relax? What did he think she was trying to do? Relaxing would be a lot easier if they weren't sticking hypo-injectors into her neck.

Zelia tried to talk. Her mouth felt like it was coated with gravel.

'Here, drink this.' A glass was pushed into her hand and she took a huge gulp.

'No,' Talen scolded her. 'Sip it!'

He sounded like her mum.

Zelia finally opened her eyes to find herself lying on a temporary bunk on the *Zealot's Heart*. They were on the bridge, near the teleporter, and *everything hurt!*

'Thank you,' she managed, passing the tumbler to Talen and catching her reflection in his eyes. She wished she hadn't. She turned sharply, the room swimming, and looked in the mirrored surface of a hull-plate. An old woman with wrinkled skin and white hair stared back. An old woman wearing Zelia's clothes.

A sob escaped Zelia's puckered lips.

'Don't panic,' Talen said quickly.

'Look at me!' she croaked, her voice like dried leaves.

'I know, but we think you're going to be okay.'

'*Think?* You don't know?'

'Why would we?' Mekki asked. 'No one has seen this... process before.'

Zelia sighed, swinging her tired legs over the side of the bunk. 'I'm sorry. It's just... scary, you know?'

Talen reached out to place a comforting hand on her arm, but stopped himself, as if he was afraid of hurting her. 'We do. Honestly.' He ran a hand through his hair, which was back to its usual colour. 'We returned to normal as soon as we got away from Grooda.'

'Then why haven't I?'

Mekki scanned her with his wrist-screen. 'You aged the most out of all of us.'

'Meaning I'm stuck like this?'

He shook his head. 'I do not think so. Your cells are regenerating, but the process is taking longer.'

'I hope you're right.' She didn't feel like she was getting younger. She felt like she was about to fall apart, but feeling sorry for herself wasn't helping anyone. 'What about Amity?' she asked.

'Amity is fine, thank you,' the captain said from the pilot's seat at the front of the flight deck. Stars were streaking past the viewport.

Zelia considered standing, but thought better of it. 'Please tell me we got what we needed?'

'The coordinates for the Emperor's Seat?' Amity checked her read-outs. 'I hope so. Mekki and Fleapit cross-referenced the path Grooda danced through the star map.'

Zelia looked across to the other side of the bridge, where the orange-furred Jokaero they called Fleapit had set up a temporary workstation.

'And?' she asked.

'And it is quite fascinating,' Mekki replied enthusiastically. 'We had to adjust the trajectory for gravitation fields and stellar anomalies...'

Zelia couldn't help but stifle a sigh.

'Perhaps you should jump to the short version,' Talen prompted.

'Really?' Mekki actually sounded disappointed.

Talen rolled his eyes. 'We found an area of space that – according to the ship's records – has been ignored for centuries.'

'Why?' Zelia asked.

'We are not sure,' Mekki replied. 'I would suggest it has been obscured by warp storms, making the region unsafe for generations.'

'Whatever the reason,' Talen added, 'the system is shrouded in a cloud of space dust so thick that sensors can't penetrate it.'

'And Pastoria's inside?'

'That's what our resident genius thinks,' Talen answered, nodding at Mekki.

Zelia attempted a weak smile. 'That's good.'

'Good?' Talen repeated. 'Zelia, it's *great*. If Pastoria is the Emperor's Seat...'

She nodded sadly. 'My mum might be there.'

Talen frowned. 'You don't sound so happy about it.'

Zelia avoided his gaze. 'I don't want her to see me like this.'

'You've looked worse.'

'Talen!'

'It's true. Show her, Mekki.'

Mekki activated his holo-projector, and Zelia looked up to see herself being carried by Talen as they raced through Rhal Screena. At least, she assumed it was her. The figure in Talen's arms looked like an ancient mummy, grey skin stretched across brittle bones.

In the past she'd been glad for Mekki's habit of recording everything that went on around her. Not any more. She looked away, not wanting to see herself.

'Zelia?'

The concern in Talen's voice was too much to take. She didn't want pity. She wanted to be back in control.

'I want to stand up,' she said, leaning on her arms to propel herself back to her feet.

'I don't think that's a good idea,' Talen told her.

She snorted, flashing him a sly smile. 'Oi! Respect your elders.'

In the end she had to accept Talen and Mekki's help. Her legs felt like jelly and her feet like lead weights, and she eased herself off the bench. Biting her lip, she took a tentative step... and then another, and another until both boys could let go.

Who would have thought that walking would seem such an achievement? She tottered towards Fleapit's bench, feeling better with every faltering step. Perhaps the others were right. Perhaps the effects of Grooda's psychic abilities were wearing off. She looked down at her hands. They still shook, but the liver spots were fading. Her vision was definitely stronger and her back seemed to be straightening as she crossed the bridge.

'Looking good,' Amity encouraged from the pilot's seat. Zelia didn't look round, concentrating instead on reaching Fleapit. On the way to Rhal Screena the Jokaero had busied himself building a small army of servo-sprites, each fashioned after Mekki's faithful robot, Meshwing, who now bobbed around Fleapit's head. The sprites lay in neat piles on the side of the workbench, waiting to be activated, while Fleapit fiddled with a small device.

'What's that?' Zelia asked.

'Ooh, is it ready?' Talen said, stepping around her. 'Can I try it first? Please? Can I?'

Fleapit rolled his eyes, but held out his hand anyway. A small silver ring sat at the centre of his palm. Talen snatched it up excitedly, slipping it over the index finger of his right hand.

'Aww,' he said, sounding disappointed. 'It's too big.'

Fleapit held up a hand to tell the ganger to wait and the ring shrank to fit snugly around Talen's finger.

'Cool!' Talen enthused, holding the ring under the light of a lume to examine it.

'Fleapit's making jewellery now?' Zelia asked.

'Not jewellery,' Talen replied, suddenly holding his arm out straight, his hand curled into a fist. 'Digi-weapons!'

He flexed his fingers and a thread of white silk shot from the ring, streaking across the flight deck to slap against the wall above the teleporter.

'It works!'

'Of course it works,' Mekki said, before explaining to Zelia. 'Grooda's spiders spun an extremely strong silk...'

'That was very difficult to get off!' Amity added from the front of the ship, rubbing the back of her right hand, which, thanks to her improving eyesight, Zelia could now see was red raw.

'Flegan-Pala analysed the silk and used it to create digi-webbers, non-fatal weapons that we can use to trap our enemies. After all, we have no way of knowing what dangers lie ahead.'

The Jokaero held out an identical ring to Zelia. She took it and slipped it over her own finger, noticing that the skin on the back of her hand was firmer than it had been a few minutes ago. As with Talen, the ring resized itself to fit her.

'Hopefully we won't need to use them,' she said, spinning it around her finger. 'Not when we reach Pastoria.'

'It never hurts to be prepared,' Talen said, continuing to spray webbing over *everything*, including Mekki, who only just managed to step out of the way in time.

'Be careful,' the Martian scolded him. 'You do not want to run out of webbing before we even make planetfall.'

Zelia flexed her hands. She'd had enough of dealing with enemies. Targian had been destroyed because the Necrons were looking for the Diadem of Transference, an ancient relic that her mum's assistant had dug up on their last expedition. Erasmus had died protecting them, but had asked Zelia to deliver the Diadem to her mother. That's what they had been trying to do these last weeks, lurching from one crisis to another as they attempted to find the mythical Emperor's Seat, where they believed Elise Lor would be waiting.

Soon, it would all be over. Soon she'd be back on her mother's ship, the *Scriptor*.

Soon she'd be home.

The *Zealot's Heart* shuddered. Zelia and the others hurried over to Amity. Both Talen and Mekki were still able to walk faster than her, but only just.

'What is it?' Talen said, sitting in the co-pilot's seat he'd adopted since they had acquired the ship.

'No wonder the planet was lost,' Amity told them as she wrestled with the usually smooth controls. 'Pastoria – if that's what it is – seems to be at the heart of a massive cloud of space dust.'

Zelia glanced up at the viewport. Amity wasn't joking. The armourglass was smeared with thick grit. It was like plunging into a nebula. 'Can we get through?'

'It shouldn't be a problem,' Amity replied, 'other than the fact that the sensors can't penetrate all this muck. For all we know we could emerge into the heart of a supernova.'

'That would not be optimal,' Mekki commented.

'You don't say.'

An alert blared on the ship's console.

'What's that?' Zelia asked.

Talen pressed a sequence of buttons, bringing up a damage report on the nearest screen. 'The dust has got into the plasma outlets.'

'We must clear them,' Mekki said.

'On it,' Talen said, pressing more controls. There was a whine somewhere deep in the ship and the shaking subsided, the alarm cutting off.

'Good work,' Amity said, and Talen

beamed at the praise. Zelia had to admit she was impressed. Talen was a far cry from the boy that had been scared to go into space when this all started.

'The dust is clearing,' he reported, checking a scope. 'We're breaking through the cloud.'

'Let's just hope we find what we're looking for,' Amity said as the viewport cleared.

Zelia's heart jumped as she saw a solitary planet ahead, orbiting a single star.

'Is that...?' She couldn't bring herself to complete the question, just in case she jinxed them.

'Let's find out,' Amity replied, taking them down.

CHAPTER FOUR

Welcome to Paradise

The contrast to Rhal Screena couldn't have been any greater. Whereas the hive world had been polluted, the air outside the city's walls thick with noxious fumes, Pastoria's brilliant blue sky was crystal clear. There were no cities or signs of industry. Vast plains rolled below them, carpeted with swaying grass to the north and thick forest to the south. According to the sensors, the air itself was clean, so much so that Amity opened the vents and let it wash through the environmental systems, replenishing the recycled oxygen they had been breathing for days. Zelia closed her eyes as she took a deep breath, the air cool and sweet.

She could hear the others talking, Talen asking if this really was the Emperor's Seat, Amity warning him not to get ahead of himself. They didn't know if Grooda had been telling the truth.

But Zelia knew. Deep in her heart, she was certain this was where her mum was waiting. She could still hear her voice, crackling over the vox as the refugee ships raced from Targian all those weeks ago.

'If I can't find you... meet at... Emperor's Seat... Do you hear me, Zelia... Emperor's Seat...'

'We're here, mum. We're here.'

Dizziness washed over Zelia, a sudden bout of vertigo that caused her to grab the back of Talen's chair.

'Zelia?'

She swallowed, her head still spinning. 'I'm fine. It... it must be the change in altitude.'

Amity glanced up. 'You're certainly looking better. This place must be agreeing with you.'

Zelia looked up, catching her reflection in a hull-plate. The captain was right. She still looked older, but only by maybe two or three years. There were circles beneath her eyes, but those had been there long before Grooda's ritual, a by-product of their recent adventures, and yes, while she looked thinner than the last time she'd seen her mum, they all did – even Mekki, who had been skinny enough in the first place. But her face was mercifully free of lines, her hair its usual black, except for a single stripe of white that swept up the front. She quite liked it, and wondered if it would stay that way.

'Let's bring her down there,' Amity said, pointing towards the peak of a small hill. Zelia gripped hard onto the seat as the *Zealot's Heart* banked, manoeuvring thrusters bringing the ship low enough for the landing gear to deploy. Usually landing had little effect on Zelia, but this time she struggled not to throw up as they came to rest, the landing struts groaning under the ship's weight.

'You do not look well, Zelia Lor,' Mekki told her as if she didn't know. She didn't respond but rushed from the ship, tottered down the ramp, her legs buckling as she reached the ground. Talen raced after her, calling out her name as she tumbled forward, throwing out her arms to stop her fall.

She knelt on all fours, fighting the nausea that threatened to overwhelm her. Talen, to his credit, didn't ask her if she was all right, but just knelt beside her, waiting for her to stop gulping air like a Catachan barking toad.

It would be a long wait. Zelia was still feeling shaky as Amity and the others stomped down the ramp, only Grunt staying on board until he was needed.

'How is she doing?' Amity asked.

'I'm fine,' Zelia all but growled at the captain.

Amity produced a bottle of pills from a coat pocket. 'Here, take one of these.'

'What are they?'

'Void-sickness capsules. They might help settle your stomach.'

Zelia thanked her, tipping a pill onto her palm. She swallowed it, wondering how long it would be before the medicine took effect.

Talen, meanwhile, had other things on his mind. 'So what now?' he asked, standing up when he was sure Zelia wasn't about to hurl. 'Where do we look?'

Mekki tapped his wrist-screen. 'I am using the *Heart*'s scrying array to scan for vapour trails in the atmosphere.'

'To search for evidence of recent air traffic.'

The Martian blinked at Talen's assessment. 'Correct.' He actually sounded impressed.

'And what have you found?'

'There are indications that void-engines have operated in the vicinity in recent weeks, a concentration of fuel particles and anti-gravitons.'

'Can we follow them?' Zelia asked, sitting rather than risking getting to her feet too soon.

'No need,' Amity grumbled, nodding towards the horizon. 'Someone's sent a welcoming party.'

Zelia jumped up and was forced to grab Talen's arm to steady herself. Amity was right. Three boxy ships were sweeping towards them. The captain pulled a vox from her belt and opened a channel.

'Hello there. This is Captain Harleen Amity of the *Profit*– I mean, of the *Zealot's Heart*. Please respond.'

The captain released the button, waiting for a reply, but none came. The only sound was the whine of the rapidly approaching engines.

The channel crackled as she tried

again. 'I repeat, this is Captain Harleen…'

Her voice fell away as they all noticed the vessels' lascannons glowing bright.

'Get down!' Talen shouted, pulling Zelia beneath the ramp. She stumbled and fell as the ships opened fire, laser bolts singeing the grass on either side of the *Heart*.

The three craft rocketed above, their passage rattling the ship's fuselage before they swung about for another pass.

'Are those refugee ships?' Talen asked, staring at the dart-shaped skimmer that led the charge.

'They do appear to be of Imperial design,' Mekki said.

'I thought these people were supposed to be your friends?' Amity said, drawing her beamer.

'So did we!' Talen said.

'We should get back on the ship,' Zelia gasped, her head spinning.

'No,' Amity insisted, aiming around the ship. 'We'll be cut to ribbons before we get back on board.'

Talen stared in disbelief at the captain's beamer. 'So you're going to try to hit them with *that?*'

'You'd rather use your spider-rings?' Amity replied.

'Digi-webbers,' Mekki corrected.

'Whatever.'

The voidships were getting closer by the second.

Talen snatched Amity's vox from her belt.

'Hey!'

He didn't waste time apologising.

'We surrender,' he shouted into the vox. 'Do you hear me? We surrender!'

Still the craft didn't reply.

'Listen, we have a sick person here. Zelia Lor. The daughter of Elise Lor. She told us to come here. I repeat, we have a sick person. We need help, not vaporising!'

All at once, the ships slammed on their air brakes. Talen took a step back as they slid to a halt in front of the *Zealot's Heart*, hanging in the air like razor-wings waiting to strike.

Amity stepped out from beneath the ramp and walked defiantly towards the craft, her weapon still raised. 'So what are you going to do? Shoot us where we stand, or show yourself?'

In answer, the craft dropped down, landing rigs unfolding. Doors opened in the side of the skimmer and a middle-aged woman jumped down. She was wearing crisp fatigues, her hair cut short with a fresh scar running down her right cheek. Her face was tanned and her eyes sharp. She walked slowly towards them, her hands raised to show she meant no harm.

'You can lower your weapon,' she told Amity, although the captain didn't comply.

'Says the woman who opened fire on us.'

The newcomer nodded at the *Zealot's Heart*. 'We didn't know if you were friend or foe.'

Mekki stepped from beneath the ramp to join the rogue trader. 'This is an Inquisitorial ship.'

The woman laughed. 'And you don't look like inquisitors! You'll have to forgive us for being a little jumpy, especially after everything that's happened. Please. We really do mean you no harm. I'm sorry we were a little hasty.'

Cautiously, Amity lowered the beamer. 'Can't say I blame you. I've been known

to shoot first and ask questions later.'
She touched the brim of her hat in greeting. 'Harleen Amity.'

The woman nodded in response. 'Kana Vrenn.' She tilted her head to see beneath the ramp. 'And these are?'

Amity introduced each of them in turn. Vrenn's eyes glistened as she heard Zelia's name.

'So you did say Lor.' She grinned warmly at Zelia. 'I know someone who will be pleased to see you.'

'You mean... my mum.'

Vrenn nodded and Zelia felt a swell of emotion that was followed immediately by another, more urgent, swell from her stomach and she finally lost her battle and threw up where she stood.

'You really aren't well,' Vrenn said, looking concerned. 'We should get you all back to Targ Outpost.'

Zelia wiped her mouth with the back of her hand. 'As in Targian?'

'We wanted to at least honour the old place,' Vrenn told her, before indicating her ship. 'Would you like to travel with me?'

'No,' Zelia said, a little too quickly, stepping closer to Amity. 'I'll go in the *Heart*.' While she was keen to see her mum, she wanted to keep close to her friends, especially while she was feeling as bad as she did. Vrenn said she understood and soon the *Zealot's Heart* was skimming over the long grass, flanked by Vrenn's ships. Zelia tried to keep watch out of the viewport but the constant motion was making her feel worse than ever.

She could hardly see by the time they landed. Dots danced across her vision as Talen helped her down the ramp, and the combination of fumes and cooling void-engines threatened to turn her stomach all over again. She tried looking around, but struggled to focus. She thought she saw a collection of domed habs, smoke curling from makeshift chimneys, but the shapes blurred together as her head spun. She knew people were talking to her, but could no longer make out the words. All she knew for sure was that there was only one thing in the increasingly distorted scene that looked remotely familiar – a planet-hopper nestled at the back of the swirling settlement.

'Is that...' she slurred, as she fell forward. 'Is that the...'

She never even felt herself hit the floor.

CHAPTER FIVE

The Plan

Zelia stirred, pulling the blanket up to her chin. She breathed in, smiling sleepily at the comforting smell of the wool and the feel of the soft pillow against her cheek.

Her eyes snapped open. The blanket. The pillow. It had to be a dream. She sat up, ignoring the now familiar whirl of vertigo. The cabin was dark, but she could make out the lines of a desk across from the bunk, her tunic thrown over the back of a chair. It was *her* desk. *Her* chair. *Her* cabin.

'Zelia.'

A sob escaped her lips at the sound of the voice. Her head jerked towards the door, bleary eyes focusing on the figure that stood at the threshold to her room. The same curly hair, now flowing over the old, battered jacket rather than pulled up into its usual bun. The same kind eyes.

'Mum!'

Zelia jumped from the bed, and ran into Elise's arms. She buried her face into her mum's chest, drenching her shirt with tears of joy. 'I found you, mum. I found you.'

'Of course you did, my clever girl,' Elise said softly, stroking her hair the way she had when Zelia was little. 'And you brought friends. I can't believe you have a Jokaero.'

Zelia allowed herself to be gently pulled out of the hug. She sniffed, nodding as she wiped her nose on the back of her hand. 'Fleapit. You'll like him, mum. He's... well, he's not always friendly, but he's looked after us. Look – he made me this.'

She showed Elise the digi-webber on her finger. Elise smiled, guiding Zelia back to her bunk. 'Mekki seems fond of him... and the ganger too.'

'Talen,' Zelia said.

'He seems nice.'

Zelia laughed. 'That's one way of putting it. We haven't always seen eye to eye, but he's brave and funny and...'

'And handsome,' Elise added.

Zelia felt herself blushing. 'I don't know about that.'

59

Elise raised a teasing eyebrow. 'Really?'

Zelia shoved her playfully. 'Mum!'

Elise laughed. 'And what about Erasmus?'

Zelia's embarrassed smile dropped away. She'd been dreading this moment, having to tell mum that her old friend was dead.

'He found something on Targian...'

'The Diadem of Transference.'

Zelia frowned. 'How did you know?'

Elise brushed hair from Zelia's face. 'Mekki told me about it. He explained it's why the Necrons destroyed Targian, and that they've been looking for it ever since.'

Zelia shifted on her bunk. If Mekki had explained about the Diadem, why hadn't he told Elise that Erasmus had sacrificed himself to save them?

'Can I see it?'

'What?'

'Can I see the Diadem?'

Zelia shook her head. 'No. Fleapit has it.'

'Then you must take me to the creature.'

'Creature?' Zelia's head had begun to throb again. 'Mum, Fleapit is my friend.'

Now it was Elise's turn to frown. 'You said it wasn't friendly.'

Zelia rubbed her aching head. 'I just meant... he can be grumpy every now and then. He's... he's not like us, that's all.'

'Not like us,' Elise repeated. Zelia swallowed. Her mouth was dry.

'Mum, can I get a glass of water or something?'

Elise shot up from the bunk. 'I can do better than that. Don't go anywhere.'

That wouldn't be an issue. All Zelia wanted to do was lie down again. Grooda's powers were taking longer to shake off than they'd thought. She looked up, trying to focus on the mirror over her desk. At least she looked more like herself. Even the streak of white had faded from her hair. If she could just get some sleep...

'Here. Drink this.'

Her mum was back, holding a steaming bowl in her hands.

'What is it?' Zelia asked as Elise sat beside her, trying not to spill any of the hot liquid. Zelia breathed in. It smelled like sweet tea.

'It'll help you feel stronger. We brew it from the local grasses.'

Zelia wrinkled her nose. 'Are you sure?'

Elise pushed the bowl towards her. 'Trust me.'

Zelia smiled. Of course she trusted her. She was her mum. She took the bowl and, raising it to her lips, blew across the liquid before taking a tentative sip. It was good, and not as hot as it had looked. She took a larger gulp, feeling warmth spread through her.

'Better?'

Zelia licked her lips and nodded. 'Actually, yeah. Better than I've been for ages.'

Elise beamed. 'I told you it would work. The crops here are incredible. The Martian boy is scanning them as we speak.'

Zelia's smile faltered. 'You mean Mekki.'

Elise nodded. 'Of course. Do you want more?'

Zelia looked down, realising she had drained the bowl. She held it out to her mother. 'That would be great. Thank you.'

'No problem at all,' Elise said, taking the bowl and rising from the bunk. 'And then you can show me the Diadem.'

It had taken another two bowls of Elise's miracle brew before Zelia had felt strong enough to leave the ship. Talen had bounded up the moment they stepped off the *Scriptor*, excitedly telling Zelia about the camp, pointing out the various dwellings that had been constructed since the refugees' arrival and the ships that formed a perimeter around the settlement.

Zelia asked her mum how she had known about the Emperor's Seat, and Elise explained how she had learned of the planet years ago when she'd dug up a cache of old scrolls on Solstice.

'The journey to Pastoria wasn't easy,' Elise admitted, 'and entering the space-cloud was a risk, but look what we found.'

Elise called a town meeting, the refugees crowding into the largest building, a prefabricated dome which Talen said reminded him of Onak's Great Hall back in Rhal Rata. Zelia sat with her friends as Elise recounted what Mekki had revealed about the true reason for Targian's destruction, and the Diadem itself.

'May we see it?' Kana Vrenn asked,

looking expectantly at Zelia.

'The Jokaero is guarding it,' Elise said, before Zelia could reply. All eyes shifted to Fleapit. He scowled back from where he had positioned himself behind Mekki.

Elise took a step towards the furry alien, holding out an expectant hand. 'Please?'

Snarling, Fleapit shot a glance at Zelia and, when she nodded, urging him to comply, reached behind his back. They heard the snap of his dimensional pack opening, and when it closed again, the metallic circlet was in his hand.

'Incredible,' Elise breathed, reaching for the crown, only for Fleapit to snatch it back, clutching the artefact close to his chest. Elise's jaw tensed. 'I would like to examine it.'

Zelia didn't need to speak Fleapit's guttural language to understand the voracity of the grunts that formed the Jokaero's reply, but Mekki translated them anyway.

'Flegan-Pala says it is too dangerous.'

Elise laughed. 'I've been handling xeno-tech for a long time, Mekki. I know what I'm doing.'

But Fleapit just shook his head, shuffling away from her.

Zelia could feel her headache returning, and wished she had more of her mother's tea. 'Fleapit, please. We agreed that we'd bring it to mum.'

The Jokaero bared his teeth.

'I can see what you mean about him,' Elise said to her daughter.

'Flegan-Pala means no offence,' Mekki cut in. 'While Zelia Lor agreed to bring the artefact to you—'

'Flegan-Pala never agreed to hand it over,' Elise said, completing his sentence.

Zelia looked surprised. 'I never knew you understood Jokaero?'

Elise never took her eyes off the circlet in Fleapit's hands. 'I know a great deal of things, now more than ever.'

Zelia felt a shiver. There was something in her mum's tone she didn't like. Something she didn't even recognise. A steely determination that she had never heard before.

Elise noticed her daughter staring at her, and sighed, rubbing a hand over her face. 'I'm sorry. It's been a difficult few weeks.'

'Tell us about it,' Talen muttered under his breath.

'I've just been so worried about you,' Elise said.

Talen frowned. 'You didn't even know me.'

'I think she meant Zelia,' Amity prompted from the bench behind him.

Talen's face flushed. 'Oh yeah, of course.'

'The question is,' Kana Vrenn said, saving Talen from further embarrassment, 'what do we do with the Diadem now?'

'An important question indeed,' Amity agreed, rising from her seat. 'And one

I should leave you to debate among yourselves.'

Talen turned back to stare at her. 'You're leaving?'

Amity spread her hands. 'I said I'd get you to the Emperor's Seat, and I have. All that remains is my payment.'

Elise's brow creased. 'Payment?'

Amity smiled politely. 'Your daughter promised me great riches for delivering her to you. Artefacts were mentioned. Maybe even a Warrant of Trade, or at least the means to obtain one?'

Kana Vrenn's hands were on her hips as she glared at the rogue trader. 'You're thinking of money at a time like this?'

Amity shrugged. 'I think of money most of the time, to be honest.'

Vrenn obviously couldn't believe what she was hearing. 'That artefact destroyed our planet.'

Beside Zelia, Mekki raised a tentative hand. 'Actually, it was the Necrons...'

'Then it must be destroyed,' a

bearded man called out from the back of the assembly. 'Before they come here.'

'I doubt you have the firepower,' Talen said. 'It's made of the same metal as the Necrons.'

'Then we should study it,' came another suggestion, this time from a dark-skinned woman on the other side of the room.

'It is too dangerous,' Mekki insisted. 'We do not even know what it does.'

'All the more reason,' the woman replied.

Before long, the gathering had descended into a noisy argument, the refugees shouting over each other to be heard. All the time, Fleapit hugged the artefact close to his chest. From his heavy scowl, Zelia could tell that the bickering wasn't helping his stubbornness. He'd never hand over the Diadem at this rate.

She stood up as an idea occurred to her. 'What if we put it back?'

Her voice cut across the crowd, who immediately fell quiet. Zelia swallowed, her cheeks burning as everyone turned to scrutinise her.

'What do you mean?' Vrenn asked.

'What I said,' Zelia replied. 'We put it back where Erasmus found it.'

Vrenn snorted. 'On Targian? I hate to remind you, child, but the hive world's gone. It's dust thanks to xenos like that.' Vrenn jabbed a finger at Fleapit, who looked like he wanted to bite it off.

Zelia stepped in front of him.
'Fleapit is *nothing* like the Necrons. And he understands more about alien technology than anyone I've ever met.' She looked apologetically at her mother. 'Even you, mum.'

Elise exhaled. 'Then what are you suggesting?'

'That we bury it, like it was buried before,' Talen said, moving forward to stand beside her. 'That's right, isn't it?'

Zelia nodded, smiling at her friend.

'Yes. It was hidden beneath the ground for thousands of years. Maybe even millions.'

'And the Necrons still found it,' Vrenn reminded her.

'Only because it was dug up,' Zelia argued. 'Perhaps being underground blocked whatever they were looking for. Perhaps it was something in the rock.'

Vrenn didn't look convinced. 'But you can't know for sure. What if we bury it, only for the Necrons to carve up Pastoria as they did Targian?'

Now Mekki stepped forward, joining the others. 'We could construct a dimensional baffle?'

Vrenn frowned. 'A what?'

'A shield,' the Martian explained. 'We built one before, when this all started.'

'And that was just using junk,' Talen added. 'This time Mekki will have better materials to work with.'

The Martian nodded. 'We could construct something like Flegan-Pala's dimensional pack.' He turned to the

Jokaero. 'Would that work? Would that hide it?'

Fleapit stuck out his bottom lip, considering this, before answering with a single grunt.

Vrenn sighed, crossing her arms across her chest. 'What do you think, Elise?'

Elise didn't take her eyes off the Jokaero. 'I think it's a great idea.'

'We'd have to find somewhere far from camp,' Vrenn rumbled.

Elise shrugged. 'We have an entire planet.'

'Although we've barely had any chance to explore it,' Vrenn admitted. 'There's still so much we don't know.'

'What about here?' Mekki said, activating a hololith of the planet.

'When did you map that?' Amity asked, peering at the flickering globe.

'When I connected to the *Heart*'s scrying array.' He pointed at a series of rocky outcrops nestled in long grass, maybe thirty or so kilometres from their current location. Mekki narrowed his eyes. 'That... that looks like blackstone.'

'We'll have to take your word for it, Cog-Boy,' Talen said.

'I think you're right,' Elise said, peering at the glowing display.

Zelia shrugged. 'And that's good... why?'

'Blackstone is incredibly rare,' Elise told her. 'And most importantly disrupts sensor sweeps.'

Mekki nodded. 'Another line of defence.'

Zelia turned back to Vrenn. 'Well?'

The older woman nodded. 'It appears we have a plan.'

CHAPTER SIX

Burial

'So, this is where you grew up, yeah?' Talen said as he glanced around the bridge. Zelia followed his gaze, looking at the bric-a-brac that covered every single surface of the *Scriptor*'s bridge.

'Yeah,' she said, bristling slightly. So the planet-hopper was a mess compared to the stark interior of the *Zealot's Heart*, but her entire life was in this ship. She could remember her parents discovering half the antiques now resting on the tarnished consoles, could still see her father bartering for the Fandro dreamcatcher that hung above the access hatch, the Fandromian stall-holder not willing to accept less than fifty gelt.

He'd eventually sold it for forty.

'I like it,' Talen said. 'It feels like home.'

Relief washed over Zelia. She hadn't realised how much she wanted Talen to like the planet-hopper, especially as the last time he'd been here, he'd been trying to rob it! But that felt like a lifetime ago, and for now, she'd decided not to mention to her mother how the two of them had met.

Elise sat at the controls, her flight seat as frayed as ever. Zelia had given up trying to persuade her to install another. She said it was comfortable and therefore it stayed... 'just like your father'. Well, at least that used to be the joke, until he had died. Now, the chair stayed because he had fitted it, back when the arm-rests didn't rattle and the upholstery wasn't covered in recaff stains.

'We're almost there,' Elise reported,

easing back on the thrusters.

Zelia slipped into the navigator's seat, reaching over to flip open a vox-channel.

'*Scriptor* to *Zealot's Heart*. Come in please.'

There was a crackle before Mekki answered from the other ship.

'*We are here, Zelia Lor.*'

'How are you getting on with the container, Mekki?'

'*Our work is almost complete. The dimensional baffle will be ready by the time we land. How are you feeling?*'

Zelia exchanged a surprised look with Talen. Empathy from the Martian! Wonders would never cease. Of course, Talen couldn't pass up an excuse to tease him.

'Careful, Mek,' he said, leaning over the back of Zelia's chair. 'You almost sound human, there.'

'*Thank you,*' came the clipped reply. '*Maybe you should try it yourself, Talen Stormweaver.*'

77

'Ooooh,' Zelia teased, giggling. 'That's gotta hurt.' Talen shook his head, smiling despite the gentle ribbing.

'I know you're missing me, Cog-Boy.'

'Like a hole in a fuel reservoir.'

Zelia snorted, although her smile faded as she glanced at her mum. Elise was staring straight ahead, seemingly oblivious to the banter. Before Targian, she would have joined in, but a lot had happened since then. Zelia's journey to Pastoria had been bad enough. She had no idea what hardships Elise and the others had endured on their way here.

There was a rumble of engines and the *Zealot's Heart* slipped past them, starting its descent.

'See you on the ground,' Zelia said, turning her attention back to the vox. 'Oh, and to answer your question, I'm feeling much better, thank you.'

'I shall prepare you a Pastorian tea,' the Martian told her before signing off. *'The restorative properties of the local flora are quite remarkable.'*

Zelia's smiled at the Martian's enthusiasm for the drink. When Zelia had told him of her mother's brew, Mekki had undertaken a detailed analysis of the ingredients, charting its various medicinal qualities.

She sat back in her chair, feeling the vibrations of the manoeuvring thrusters as Elise brought the *Scriptor* down into a clearing between the rocks. While it was great being home, she was surprised to realise how strange it was not to have Mekki and Fleapit with them. The Jokaero had insisted on taking the *Zealot's Heart*, Mekki explaining it was due to the *Heart*'s superior equipment, but Zelia suspected that Fleapit felt safer on Amity's ship. Everything was changing so fast. It was only natural that they were feeling jumpy, Fleapit included.

Zelia allowed herself a moment to close her eyes and feel the warmth of the sun on her skin as she stepped down the ramp. Amity was helping

Vrenn unload a portable mining rig that the older woman had brought on her own ship, the dart-shaped skimmer that had threatened them when they first arrived. Before long, the mobile drill was boring down into the hard ground, churning up mud as they prepared the Diadem's final resting place.

'How deep should we go?' Zelia asked.

'I would say at least five times the depth of our dig on Targian,' Mekki said, appearing behind her. 'That, and the blackstone, should give enough protection.'

Zelia hoped he was right as Fleapit emerged from the *Heart*, pushing a grav-crate that Zelia assumed contained the Diadem. They walked towards the rig, the drill rising to swing clear, but Fleapit suddenly stopped, his lips drawn back into a snarl.

'What's wrong with him?' Talen asked.

Zelia didn't know, but could see the hair bristling on the alien's shoulders. Something had spooked him.

Amity joined them, repeating Talen's question. Mekki activated his wrist-screen, glancing up from the display to peer at the trees.

The rogue trader put her weight on one hip, crossing her arms. 'Let me guess — you're taking advantage of my ship's scryers again.'

'*Your* ship?' Talen said, mirroring her pose. 'I seem to remember that I was the one who got us on board. Seems to me that I'm the captain.'

Amity shared a conspiratorial smile with the young ganger. 'In your dreams, hotshot. So, what is it, Mekki?'

The Martian looked up from his reading, obviously satisfied. 'Nothing. As far as I can tell we are the only life forms for kilometres around.'

'But you said the rock could block signals.'

'That is true, Zelia Lor,' Mekki confirmed. 'But we would have noticed any other ships on our approach.'

Talen peered between the jagged rocks

that jutted up from the tall grass. 'Do you think it's a wild animal?'

But the only creature growling was Fleapit. In fact, Zelia suddenly realised that she couldn't hear any other wildlife. There had been birds in the air when they had arrived, and insects chirping in the grass beneath their feet. Now everything was silent. She shivered, rubbing her arms. Had it got colder?

'What's the hold-up?' It was Vrenn, walking over from the drilling rig where Elise waited. 'You wanted a hole. We dug you a hole.'

Zelia approached Fleapit cautiously. She knew the Jokaero wouldn't hurt her, but had never seen him so spooked before.

'Fleapit? The sooner we bury the Diadem, the sooner we can put this all behind us.'

'Yeah,' Talen added. 'Just think of all the machines you could build for the refugees once we've got rid of that thing.' He leant in closer, lowering his voice. 'Not to mention a few stupidly powerful weapons...'

Fleapit chuckled at the thought.

'That's the spirit,' Talen said. 'Maybe we could find something to blow up!'

'Talen!' Zelia scolded.

The ganger smirked, nodding at Fleapit as he continued trudging towards the borehole. 'It worked, didn't it? Sometimes you need to speak his language.'

'And I thought I was the only one who could communicate with Flegan-Pala,' Mekki said as they reached the rig.

Zelia looked down into the pit, feeling her stomach flip. She reached out for her mum, but instead found Talen, who grabbed her arm.

'Don't fall in.'

'I'll try not to.'

'How deep is it anyway?' asked Amity.

Mekki checked his screen. 'Two hundred metres.'

'As instructed,' Vrenn said, rubbing her hands together to warm them. It wasn't just Zelia, then. The air had definitely cooled.

'So?' Talen prompted.

But Fleapit wasn't listening. His scowl had returned and along with it, his growl. He looked up as a rumble rolled across the sky.

'Is that thunder?' Mekki asked.

Zelia shook her head. 'No,' she replied. 'It sounded like…'

'Like engines,' Amity said as a shadow passed over them. The trees shook around them, leaves falling to the ground as a shape loomed in front of the sun, a gigantic black square blocking out the meagre warmth that Zelia had enjoyed moments before. It grew larger, dropping down from above, and Zelia felt a cold shiver as she reached for her omniscope. She didn't want to believe what she saw when she looked through the lens, the scope's internal cogitator immediately recognising the dark green metal. They were looking at the bottom of a giant pyramid: a huge, terrible pyramid made of the same material as the Doom Scythes that had attacked Targian.

The Necrons had followed them to Pastoria.

CHAPTER SEVEN

Tomb Blades

'They won't do any good,' Talen yelled as Amity aimed her blasters at the rapidly descending craft.

'They've come for the Diadem,' she barked. 'Get it back on the *Heart*.'

It was as if the Necrons had heard her. Emerald lightning lanced from the ship, carving into the ground between them and Amity's ship.

'It's no good,' Elise yelled, spinning around to face Fleapit. 'We won't be able to outrun them. Give the relic to me.'

'What are you going to do with it?' Zelia asked as Fleapit pulled the grav-crate towards him.

'Take it into the rocks,' her mother replied. 'Mekki was right. The blackstone must have shielded the Necrons' approach. Maybe the rock will confuse whatever sensors they use.'

'Nice idea,' Talen said, looking up, 'but will it confuse them?'

Sickle-shaped Necron jetbikes were streaming out of a hatch in the underside of the craft, each piloted by a grinning metal skeleton.

'Look out,' Vrenn said, pushing Zelia

aside as the nearest Necron opened fire, green energy bursting from the oversized weapon that hung beneath the circular fighter. Zelia stumbled and fell, looking up to see a smoking crater where Vrenn had been seconds before. The woman had been vaporised!

'Change of plan,' Elise shouted, pulling Zelia to her feet and pushing her towards their ship. 'Everyone on board the *Scriptor*. We won't be able to outrun Tomb Blades on the ground, but may be able to give them the slip in the air.'

'Tomb Blades?' Zelia asked as she was dragged along.

'The jetbikes,' Elise snapped.

'Yeah, and what about that thing?' Talen said, glancing up at the pyramid as he ran.

'One problem at a time,' Amity said, Mekki and Fleapit running alongside her. 'You take Talen and Zelia in the *Scriptor*. I'll follow on with the others.'

'And the Diadem,' Mekki pointed out

as he kept pace with the Jokaero.

'No!' Elise snapped. 'They'll be safer with me.'

There was no time to argue as the lead Tomb Blade strafed the ground between the two ships. Amity cried out as she was thrown into the air, thudding to the scorched dirt near the *Zealot's Heart*.

The emerald bolts kept coming, forcing Fleapit and Mekki to head to the *Scriptor* after all, with its boarding ramp already lowered.

But Talen didn't come with them. He ducked sizzling disintegrator beams to race to Amity's side.

'Talen!' Zelia shouted out, but was grabbed by Mekki and hauled up the boarding ramp. Fleapit and Elise were already on board, but Zelia couldn't see Talen or Amity through the haze of green smoke.

'We can't leave him,' she said, pulling her arm free.

'Talen Stormweaver would not want

you to get killed,' Mekki told her, grabbing her again and pulling her towards the hatch.

In the end, she didn't have a choice. Vrenn's skimmer took a direct hit, the fuel tank igniting and the speeder dissolving into a ball of flames. The force of the blast threw Zelia and Mekki across the threshold, and before they could even scramble to their feet, Elise had fired the engines.

The *Scriptor* lurched into the sky, the boarding ramp still open. Mekki ran to the controls as a Tomb Blade flew straight at them. Green energy spat from its disintegrator, streaking past Zelia to strike Elise's grav-bike, which was docked in its usual spot in the *Scriptor*'s hold.

Not any more. The bike dissolved into a blaze of green fire, the battery rupturing as particle beam met Imperial fuel cells. Zelia was thrown back, tumbling down the still-gaping boarding ramp. Crying out, she scrabbled to stop herself plummeting down into the forest, finally grabbing hold of the ramp as her legs disappeared over the edge. She dragged herself up, glancing over her shoulder to see the Tomb Blade almost upon them. She could see the pilot's glowing green eyes and rictus grin, almost feel the heat from its disintegrator cannon.

She yelled at Mekki to raise the ramp as she inched back into the ship, but instead the Martian dashed to her, pulling her back into the hold himself.

'The hydraulics were damaged in the explosion,' he shouted over the roar of the wind and the planet-hopper's engines. 'It will not shut. If we can seal the internal door...'

They ran across the hold towards the bulky door that led into the bowels of the ship, diving across the threshold and slamming it shut. They couldn't help but glance through the thick glass at the approaching Tomb Blade, the muzzle of its particle beamer glowing bright as it prepared to unleash fresh destruction. At this range, it would slice through the heart of the ship, ripping the *Scriptor* in two!

CHAPTER EIGHT

Shadowlooms

Zelia knew she had to run. Of course she did. But even as Mekki took to his heels, calling her name, she stood rooted to the spot, transfixed by the Necron that was about to cause their destruction. She couldn't believe that it would end like this, blown apart by one solitary Necron. So much for the Emperor protecting them. So much for the hope she had kept burning since Targian had been destroyed.

It had all been for nothing.

No. That wasn't true. Hope wasn't lost.

As Zelia watched, the Necron prepared

to fire. She could see its finger almost on the trigger when the jetbike exploded! Zelia screwed her eyes up against the sudden glare and when she opened them again saw the *Zealot's Heart* flying right behind them. Amity had escaped the carnage in the wood. And if she had survived then maybe Talen had too!

Zelia raced to the front of the planet-hopper, the thudding of her feet on the deck-plates matching the pounding of her own heart. She burst into the bridge as Talen's voice came over the vox.

'*Scriptor, come in please.*'

Zelia laughed in relief. 'Talen, you're alive.'

'*It's going to take more than a few Necrons to kill me.*'

'A few?'

She could almost hear his smile. '*They're not so tough.*'

Mekki was sitting at a terminal to the side of the main console, scrolling through images from the ship's rear picters. The displays showed the *Zealot's Heart* flying behind them, a phalanx of Tomb Blades in pursuit. In the distance, the main Necron craft hung impossibly in the air.

From this angle, Zelia could make out more of the terrifying pyramid. Cannons jutted out of its sloped sides, a giant crystal pulsating at its peak, but Zelia's eye was drawn to the sigil burning just beneath the massive emerald, a symbol Zelia remembered all too well. She had last seen it on the chest of the Necron Hunter that had killed Erasmus, and before that on the wings of the Doom Scythes that had carved up Rhal Rata. That settled it. These were the same Necrons that had destroyed Targian.

The *Zealot's Heart* lurched as a particle beam sliced across her hull. Zelia heard Talen gasp over the vox.

'That was close.'

'Still think they're not so tough?' Zelia asked, as Fleapit crouched beneath a cogitator terminal, the Diadem's crate clutched to his chest.

'We'll hold them off,' Amity said over the channel. *'You get away from Pastoria.'*

'We cannot, Harleen Amity,' Mekki said. 'The rear hatch is jammed open. We would be exposed to the void as soon as we broke orbit.'

'Then head back to the settlement and get on a different ship.'

'What about you?' Zelia asked.

'We'll follow you as soon as we've shot more of these Throne-forsaken jetbikes out of the sky.'

'Such an outcome is unlikely,' Mekki intoned. 'My scans indicate that the Tomb Blades – and most probably the pyramid – are comprised of the same living metal as the Necrons themselves. It will repair almost as soon as it is damaged.'

'Thanks, Mekki,' Amity replied. *'That's a* real *help. Just get to safety and we'll see you later.'*

Zelia looked to the screens to see the *Zealot's Heart* drop into a loop, its laser cannons firing as it swept up from below to engage the Tomb Blades.

'They don't stand a chance, do they?' she said as more jetbikes streamed from the ship.

'No,' came her mother's matter-of-fact reply. Zelia glared at her mum. She didn't want her to agree. She wanted her to say it was all going to be all right, that they would escape the Necrons, that she would see her friends again.

'Something is happening,' Mekki announced. She looked over his shoulder to see inky clouds emerging from the heart of each Tomb Blade, obscuring the fighters, although there was no mistaking the green particle beams that blasted out of the dark patches.

'What are they?' Zelia asked.

Elise didn't even look up from the controls as she replied. 'Shadowlooms.'

'What?'

'Portable black-light generators that can shield Tomb Blades, making it impossible to predict their angle of approach. The looms will eventually combine, plunging the *Zealot's Heart* into darkness.'

Sure enough, the dark auras were bleeding into each other, blocking out the picter's view of both the *Heart* and the ship beyond.

'Perhaps that is how the pyramid hid its own approach,' Mekki mused, trying to adjust the sensors to compensate.

'Surely we would have seen something that large?'

Mekki shrugged. 'Some kind of cloaking device, maybe.'

Zelia shook her head. How could Mekki be so calm, so clinical? And wasn't he missing the bigger question?

'How do you know so much about the Necrons?' Zelia asked her mother. 'First "Tomb Blades" and now "Shadowlooms"?'

Elise continued to look straight ahead.

'I had plenty of time for research while waiting for you. There were records in the *Scriptor*'s databanks, from past excavations.'

'Really?' Something about that didn't ring true. Zelia looked to Mekki. 'Have you ever heard these names before?'

The Martian considered the question before slotting his fingers into an access port on the terminal, his haptic connectors clicking into place. The electoos on his head flashed as he accessed the *Scriptor*'s records, his brow knitting into a frown behind its collection of lenses.

'There is no mention of Tomb Blades or Shadowlooms in the ship library,' he reported. 'Although there are plenty of texts that have yet to be digitised.'

That was true enough. Books and scrolls were heaped in piles all over the ship, but something didn't seem right. Zelia knew it in her gut.

'We can talk about this later,' Elise said, but Zelia wasn't having that, even with a battle raging behind them.

'No. We can talk about it now.'

In answer, Elise threw the ship into a sharp turn, forcing Zelia to grab hold of Mekki's chair to stop herself being chucked across the deck.

'What are you doing?' Zelia asked, as they levelled out to fly back towards the fight.

'Helping our friends,' came the reply.

'Amity told us to get away.'

'You are worried about Talen,' Elise said.

'I'm more concerned that you're flying into battle without activating what little defences we have.'

'The *Scriptor* has no weapons,' Mekki reminded her.

'Exactly. Then what can we do to help the *Heart*?'

'We can confuse the enemy,' Elise said sharply, as the planet-hopper plunged into the Shadowlooms' murky darkness. 'They won't be expecting us to attack.'

Zelia stared at the solid black on the

other side of the viewport. 'What if we hit something?'

'Maybe that is the idea?' Mekki suggested, as the *Scriptor* emerged on the other side of the cloud, heading straight for the pyramid. Tomb Blades dropped into formation on either side of the ship, but didn't attack. Instead, they flew alongside, like an escort.

Elise accelerated, the *Scriptor* picking up speed, the Necrons matching the planet-hopper's velocity. They were going to ram the pyramid!

'Mum,' Zelia cried out as the huge ship loomed closer than ever. 'Don't.'

She made a grab for the flight stick, but Elise struck out, the blow sending Zelia flying across the bridge. She crashed back to the floor and skidded to a halt.

Never mind that her mum had just hit her, how had she got so strong?

Mekki twisted his haptic connectors in the access point.

'What are you doing?' Elise bellowed

as her controls went dead.

'Turning us around,' Mekki said, having seized control of the *Scriptor*. He turned his head, and the ship turned with it, banking to the left and smashing into the Tomb Blades that flanked their port side. The planet-hopper shuddered as explosions blossomed across its hull, the engines complaining as they struggled to correct their course. They were still slewing towards the pyramid's all-too-solid walls.

Mekki was doing his best, but it was too late.
They were going to crash!

CHAPTER NINE

The Truth

Zelia screwed up her eyes, convinced they were going to smash into the pyramid at any moment. The explosion never came. Instead a screeching noise filled her ears, accompanied by green light which flashed through her eyelids.

She opened her eyes to see the *Scriptor*'s flight deck dissolve in an emerald storm. Zelia screamed as she felt her body stretch, the deck disappearing beneath her feet. Is this what a Necron disintegrator beam felt like? Was every atom in her body blasting apart, the skin stripped from her bones as her skeleton turned to dust?

Even her scream was lost in the cacophony, just one more noise in the chaos that swirled around her.

And then the world crashed back into view. Blurred images danced in front of her eyes, and every nerve in her body felt frayed, but she could feel metal beneath her feet again. She breathed in, finding the air notably cooler. She shook her head, not just to clear her vision, but also her ears. Something was definitely wrong with them, the squeal of the *Scriptor*'s engines replaced by a deep mechanical pulse, like a heartbeat she could feel in the pit of her stomach.

'Mum?' she croaked, barely recognising her own voice as her eyes started to make sense of the kaleidoscope of colours that assaulted her senses. She could see Fleapit, still clutching the crate, and Mekki, sprawled on the floor near her. Her mother was standing in front of them all, and Zelia could finally make out that they were all on a raised metal dais.

There was someone else, a tall figure, standing just in front of the platform. Zelia cried out as it came into focus: the fixed grin, the single eye, the heavy beamer-rifle held in taloned hands.

There was nothing to prove it was the same Necron that had hunted them on the ice planet following Targian's destruction, nothing but the certainty that crawled in Zelia's gut. The

Hunter had repaired itself following the avalanche, but its metal skin was pitted, a deep dent tarnishing its once smooth skull. Maybe Erasmus's sonic mine had interfered with the Hunter's regenerative abilities or maybe it was wearing the scars of their previous encounter as trophies.

'Where are we?' she squeaked, still disorientated.

'You know full well, child,' her mother said, turning to face her. 'On the Necron Monolith. We were teleported here before the *Scriptor* crashed.'

Zelia looked around. As far as she could see there was no damage. She had no way of knowing whether the *Scriptor* had rammed into the pyramid or spiralled to the ground, but she knew someone who would.

Jumping to her feet, she activated the vox stitched into her jacket, broadcasting on every channel she could.

'This is Zelia Lor. We have been

captured by the Necrons. Run for your lives. Get off Pastoria. It isn't safe.'

She didn't even see her mum move. One minute, Elise was standing at the far end of the teleport pad and the next she was in Zelia's face. Her hand shot forward, her fingers closing around Zelia's vox and squeezing. The vox crunched like a broken toy as it was destroyed in Elise's hand, fragments tinkling to the ground when she released her grip.

'What are you?' Zelia said as she saw a faint green glow behind her eyes.

'I am a servant of the Necrons,' came the impossible reply. 'As are you, my child.'

CHAPTER TEN

Mindshackle

'This is Zelia Lor. We have been captured by the Necrons. Run for your lives. Get off Pastoria. It isn't—'

Zelia's message cut off, not that Talen had been able to concentrate on her words in the first place. Night seemed to have fallen around the *Zealot's Heart*. It was pitch-black outside the viewport and the sensors were next to useless, the scry-signals bouncing off whatever cloud the Tomb Blades were generating.

But Amity wasn't giving up. She hadn't given up when she had scrabbled from the ground, still dazed

113

from the particle beam, and shoved Talen towards the *Heart*. She hadn't given up when she'd shot into the sky after the *Scriptor*, taking out the Necron jetbike that threatened to blow the planet-hopper to pieces.

And she hadn't given up as every Tomb Blade they hit miraculously repaired itself, returning to the fight minutes after being blasted from the air.

The ship shook as it took more fire, the Tomb Blades barely more than green streaks in the gloom of the shadow field. Lume-globes exploded in the ceiling, sparks raining from above as Amity swung the ship from left to right, a moving target always more difficult to hit – not that it seemed to slow the Necron attack. Meshwing was trying to repair the ship's systems as quickly as they shut down, while Grunt extinguished fires in the rear stations, and still the particle beams kept coming.

His teeth gritted, Talen mashed his triggers, sending las-bolts streaming into the swirling darkness.

'This is hopeless,' Amity said. 'We don't stand a chance in this fog.'

'But what about Zelia and the others?' Talen asked, holding on to avoid being thrown from his station.

'You heard her,' Amity replied matter-of-factly. 'They've been captured. It's too late. We need to pull out.'

'What are you doing?' Talen cried out as Amity brought the ship about and rocketed out of the Tomb Blades' shroud.

'Getting us out of here.'

'We're running away?' Talen turned to the screens, switching to the view of the pyramid behind them. There was no sign of the *Scriptor*, save for an ominous plume of smoke rising from a cluster of trees below.

'We're not running away,' Amity corrected him, firing the engines to put as much distance as possible between them and the Monolith. 'We're coming up with a new strategy.'

'One that involves running away!' Talen couldn't believe this was happening. 'We can't leave them in that thing.'

Amity whirled around to face him, never taking her hand off the flight stick. 'What exactly do you want me to do? Turn around and attempt a rescue?'

'Yes!'

'And what happens if by some miracle we get past the Tomb Blades? What do we do then, eh? Attack a Necron battle station single-handed? Did you see the size of those cannons?'

'But Zelia...'

'We won't be able to do a single thing to help Zelia if we get destroyed. Yes, Talen, we're retreating, but we're retreating back to the camp – a camp that no doubt has weapons. We can't help Zelia on our own, that's just a fact. But if we can persuade the refugees to lend a hand, there's a chance – a very small chance – that we might be able to save her.'

Zelia felt numb as they were marched into a vast chamber at the top of the pyramid.

Her mum was working with the Necrons.

The Necrons!

Zelia had lost track of the times she'd dreamt of being reunited with her mother over the last few weeks, of delivering the Diadem into her hands, as Erasmus had asked.

'Stop,' Elise barked, and Zelia obeyed almost without thinking. She looked up to see they had been brought in front of a majestic throne, which towered over them at the top of a flight of emerald steps. A Necron glared down at them, the largest Necron Zelia had ever seen. It was clad in bulky armour, a golden headdress sweeping down into its metallic spine and a twin-bladed staff clasped in a gauntleted hand.

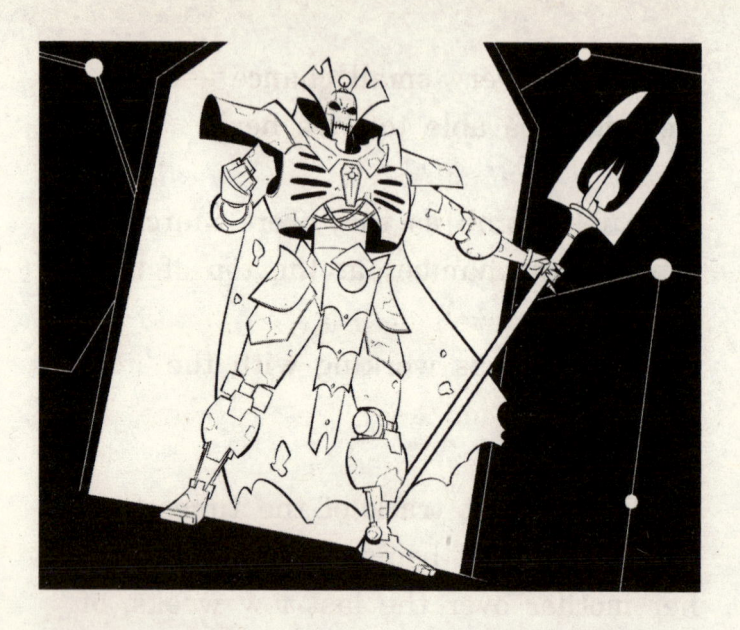

Necron guards stood at either side of it, a legion of the vile creatures lined up behind them, particle disintegrators in hand.

'Overlord Merlek,' Elise said, bowing low before the skeletal ruler. 'I bring you the keepers of the Diadem.'

'You have done well, fleshling,' the Overlord replied, his voice low and grating. He turned his green gaze towards the one-eyed Necron that stood directly behind Zelia. 'As have you, my Hunter.'

The Hunter barely responded, nodding sharply in acknowledgement.

'How did you find us?' Mekki cried out beside her. Fleapit stood behind the daring Martian. Despite their situation, Zelia felt a swell of pride at Mekki's words. A few weeks ago, Mekki would have barely said boo to a bogworm and yet here he was standing defiantly in front of a Necron lord.

And if Mekki could do it, then so could she!

'Yes,' she shouted, stepping up beside him. 'Tell us.'

'You are in no position to make demands,' Merlek intoned.

'You have hounded us across the galaxy,' Zelia called out, trying her best not to stammer in fear. 'We deserve an explanation.'

Zelia knew she was playing with promethium. If she were here, Amity would no doubt tell her standing up against a Necron was pointless, foolish even, but she had to try. If she didn't, she would lose part of herself, the best part. She would lose hope.

She tensed, expecting energy to lance down from the Overlord's power staff. Instead the Necron brought the metal rod down with a sharp crack. Suddenly the air was alive with hololiths. The Hunter stalking them through the snowy forest after they'd escaped the Necron fleet. Fleapit firing his strange sonic weapon. Erasmus standing on the side of an icy mountain. Tears welled in Zelia's eyes as she saw the old man, standing defenceless in front of the Hunter before a wall of snow dashed them against a rock.

She winced as she heard Erasmus's voice, screaming into a vox. *'Get the Diadem to Elise. She'll know what to do with it.'*

Zelia glanced back to the Hunter. It had survived the avalanche and had Erasmus's last words burned into its memory.

'But that doesn't explain how you

found Pastoria,' she said, looking up at the Overlord. 'Were you following us all the time? Is that how you did it? Did you place a tracer on our ship?'

'That was not necessary,' Merlek said. 'We know all.' There was no pride in his robotic voice. It was a statement of fact, nothing more.

His staff came down for a second time. 'Behold, the might of the Necrons.'

The scenes changed again. Zelia saw ships blasting from Rhal Rata, fleeing into the stars, cut down one by one by Necron fighters. Explosions. Burning metal. Bodies frozen in the void.

All around, cries for help echoed around the chamber – voices from the crippled ships calling for the Emperor's protection, tears and screams masked by explosions and fire.

And above it all, one particular voice echoing across the devastation.

'If I can't find you... meet at... Emperor's Seat...'

Her blood turned cold.

'Do you hear me, Zelia... Emperor's Seat...'

Zelia glared at Elise Lor through her tears. How long had she been working for the Necrons? Had this all been part of their plan?

The Necrons hadn't tracked the Diadem. There had been no need. Thanks to her mum's message, they knew exactly where Zelia was heading. To the Emperor's Seat. All they had to do was find it and wait for Zelia and the others to catch up.

To bring them their prize.

To bring *Elise* their prize.

They had found her mum and changed her in some way, made her work for them. All to set a trap.

The recordings were increasing in volume, overlapping, distorting, a wall of sound.

Help us.

Protect us.

Meet at the Emperor's Seat.

'Please,' Zelia yelled, clamping her

hands over her ears. 'I've heard enough. I've heard enough!'

Everything went quiet. The messages were gone, the hololiths too. Merlek glared coldly down at them. The explanation hadn't been a kindness. It was a lesson, a reminder that resistance was useless.

That the Necrons had already won.

Elise strode towards Fleapit and made a grab for the crate. The Jokaero tried to resist, but Elise was too strong. The alien ape gasped as she crushed the container with her bare hands, the lid buckling before springing open. How was she doing this?

It didn't matter, though. Zelia couldn't help but smile as Elise threw the crate across the throne room. It clattered on the polished floor, sliding to a stop, its contents exposed for all to see.

The crate was empty.

'Where is the relic?' Merlek demanded.

'Somewhere you'll never find it,' Zelia said, realising what Fleapit had done.

Elise turned to her master. 'The Jokaero has an inter-dimensional storage device mounted on its back. It must have transferred the relic during the flight.'

'Then recover it!' the Overlord commanded.

Fleapit blew a raspberry.

This time Zelia laughed out loud. She couldn't help herself. The Necrons could do what they wanted to them, but Fleapit was the only creature who could open the dimensional backpack. If he didn't want it open, the Diadem would be locked away forever.

The Necrons had lost, after all.

Hadn't they?

Zelia's smile fell away as two Necron guards broke rank and stomped over to Fleapit, grabbing his arms. He tried to struggle, but there was no escape. Both Zelia and Mekki moved to help, but were forced to skid to a halt as rows of disintegrators zeroed in on them.

'You will open the pack,' Elise commanded.

Fleapit shook his head.

'That wasn't a request,' she told him.

Its joints clanking, the Hunter stalked towards Fleapit. Its mouth yawned open and something scrambled out, a small metal scarab that ran down the Hunter's body, jumping off the Necron's feet to scuttle towards Fleapit.

The Jokaero struggled against his captors, kicking out as the metal insect crawled up his leg, disappearing into the fur on his back. The Necrons let go and Fleapit flailed in front of them, scratching frantically, trying to dislodge the scarab which was buried in his fur.

There was a sudden crunch, like mechanical jaws closing, and Fleapit's arms went limp, his hands thudding to the floor like a puppet whose strings had been cut. For a second, his mouth went slack, his eyelids drooping, before the Jokaero seemed to recover. He stood upright, his back cracking as it straightened, his posture better than ever. However, it was the expression on his face that sent gooseflesh crawling across Zelia's skin.

Fleapit's expression was blank, his face an impassive mask. When he finally opened his eyes, they throbbed with sickly green light.

'No,' Zelia whimpered as the Jokaero calmly reached behind his back, opened the dimensional pack and removed the Diadem.

Merlek sat forward eagerly. 'Bring it to me.'

Elise took the relic from the brainwashed Jokaero and slowly, ceremoniously ascended the steep stairs to the throne, the Diadem held in both hands.

Beside Zelia, Mekki snapped a telescopic lens over one of his eyes and peered at the back of Elise's head.

'Zelia Lor – look!'

Zelia was in no mood for guessing games. 'What is it, Mekki?'

'On the back of her neck. Do you see?'

Worried that the Necrons would think she was going for a weapon, Zelia gingerly reached for her omniscope. No one moved, their glowing eyes fixed on the tableau before them, and so, still expecting to be blasted any second, she quietly unfolded the scope and squinted through the lens.

A glint of silver beneath her mother's hair caught her breath. She zoomed in, and confirmed the worst. A row of metal legs were clamped to Elise's neck.

'Elise Lor is not working for the Necrons,' Mekki whispered. 'She is *enslaved* by them, her mind shackled by a scarab.'

Zelia lowered the omniscope. 'Just like Fleapit.'

Elise *hadn't* betrayed them. She'd really thought the Emperor's Seat was a safe haven and had no idea that the Necrons were listening, or that they'd be waiting for her, ready to transform her into their pawn.

And now she was handing a weapon of unimaginable power to the Necron Overlord. Zelia stopped herself from bolting up the steps as Merlek wrapped his metal fingers around the artefact she'd protected for so long. It would be a pointless sacrifice. The Necron guards were poised, ready to fire upon anyone who threatened their lord.

Merlek rose, holding the crown in the air.

'This is it,' he announced. 'The

moment we have been waiting for. Set course for the human settlement. The Transference must begin immediately!'

CHAPTER ELEVEN

No Escape

Targ Outpost was in chaos. Refugees were running for their ships, taking off the moment the hatches were closed.

'Why won't they listen?' Talen said as he watched the settlers abandon their habs and take to the skies, anything to avoid the Tomb Blades that were screaming through the air towards them.

'Because they're scared,' Amity said, watching the first ships leave. 'And I can't blame them.'

That hadn't stopped her trying to persuade them to fight as soon as the *Zealot's Heart* had touched down, but no one would listen. Talen shielded his eyes against the noonday sun to watch a battered cruiser disappear into the clouds. It had been the first ship to leave, a father bundling his family into its hold. At least they had got away... or so Talen thought. Suddenly there was a flash of green light followed by an explosion, and the burning hull of the escaping craft plummeted from the heavens.

Talen gasped as he saw Tomb Blades following the wreckage down, their weapons trained on the unmistakable shape of an escape pod. The family must have jettisoned before the explosion, only to be tracked by the Necrons, who for some reason seemed content to escort the escape pod back to the ground. Talen heard its landing thrusters fire, attempting to slow its descent, before it thudded into the earth, sending up a cloud of dirt.

The Tomb Blades peeled off to target another cruiser, emerald lightning slicing into its thrusters. The rockets blew out and the heavy vessel's nose dipped, crashing into a habitation dome.

All around, the fleeing ships were brought down, Tomb Blades swarming around them like hornets, although unlike the escape from Targian none of them were being atomised.

'They're just targeting their propulsion systems,' Talen realised.

Amity nodded. 'Making sure they can't leave.'

As the last ship crashed back to the ground, the Necrons turned on the refugees, but instead of blowing them to pieces, they swept around to herd the frightened humans together, warning shots churning up the mud at their feet if they tried to run.

'Why aren't they being vaporised?' Talen asked, as a Necron noticed him and Amity standing in the shadow of the *Zealot's Heart*. The rogue trader raised a beamer and snapped off a salvo of las-blasts at the grinning pilot as it swooped towards them.

'Who cares? Get back on the ship!'

No chance. The Necron skidded past them, the Tomb Blade's anti-gravs whining as it positioned itself in front of the ramp. Talen and Amity froze, waiting for particle beams that never came, as the Necron hunched over its controls.

'What is it waiting for?' Talen cried out, rooted to the spot. A Necron flyer swept above, a bomber similar to the crescent-shaped fighters that had attacked Rhal Rata. The ordnance bays sprang open, but instead of bombs, tiny Necron scarabs rained down on the settlement. Talen jumped back as one landed near him. He'd seen what the metal creatures had done on Targian, devouring entire voidships within seconds. He yelled in surprise as a well-aimed blast from Amity's beamer reduced the hideous insect to scrap, only for the scorched parts to start rebuilding.

He spun on his heels, not sure where to run. Amity was wheeling around, picking off as many of the scurrying pests as she could, but there were just too many. They were scampering everywhere, swarming onto the backs of the settlers, who frantically tried to brush them away. But for every scarab that was knocked clear there was another that clamped itself at the base of a refugee's neck, the human freezing for a moment before walking calmly – *too* calmly – towards the centre of the small town. They were like sleepwalkers, their eyes glowing green, minds blank.

No. They weren't blank. They had been taken over by the scarabs. *That's* why the Necrons had only scuttled the ships, rather than destroying them outright. They needed the settlers for some reason.

'Talen! Look out! Your arm!'

Talen looked down at Amity's warning, crying out as he saw a scarab scrambling up his shirt sleeve, its cyclopean eye glowing a sickly green. He swiped at it, knocking the cybernetic bug to the ground, where it landed on its back, segmented legs clawing the air. Talen kicked it as hard as he could, and the scarab arced through the air to be destroyed by a swift blast from Amity. The rogue trader was a blur, coat-tails flying as she spun and fired, spun and fired. Talen had never felt so hopeless. He had no weapon and nowhere to run.

No. That wasn't true. He did have a weapon.

Talen raised his digi-webber in the direction of a scuttling scarab and squeezed his fist. A stream of synthetic spider-silk shot out, plastering the scarab to the ground.

He laughed, turning and firing again, although this time his aim wasn't half as good and he missed his target. He readjusted his arm and tried again, snaring another scarab that had been scuttling greedily towards Amity. Yes! He was back in the game... but for how long?

He'd forgotten about the Tomb Blade that was blocking the *Zealot's Heart*. It shot forward with an ear-piercing scream, heading straight for him. Talen threw himself to the ground, and the sickle-shaped jetbike streaked over him, the barrel of its disintegrator cannon brushing his back. He looked up, his mouth full of dirt, and saw the Necron flyer close on Amity. It hadn't been after Talen at all. It wanted the rogue trader.

Talen scrambled up, squeezing off more webbing, but the jetbike was out of range. Amity turned, firing at the Necron, but it was no good. The alien grabbed her, its mount pulling up. Amity was lifted high into the air. She twisted, firing at the Necron, but the pilot kicked out with a steel boot, catching Amity in the head.

'No!' Talen cried out as her body went limp, her beamers slipping from her hands to land near his feet. He scooped them up, but could only watch as the unconscious rogue trader was carried towards the approaching pyramid.

CHAPTER TWELVE

Trapped Souls

'Just stay out of the way, will you?'

Talen batted Meshwing away. The servo-sprite had been flapping nervously around his head the moment he'd raced back on board the *Zealot's Heart*. He'd raised the ramp and hurried through to the bridge, activating the picters to see what was happening outside.

The answer was... nothing.

The settlers were all standing in a group at the centre of the camp, all facing the pyramid that was slowly approaching. The Necrons meanwhile were scouting back and forth on their Tomb Blades, the few remaining scarabs scuttling around like metal cockroaches, searching for fresh minds to enslave.

Talen glanced at the flight controls behind him. He'd learned a lot from Amity, but doubted he could take off by himself. Of course there was Grunt, standing motionless beside the door as always, but the mindless servitor was little more than a machine. There's no way he'd be able to help Talen pilot the ship. And as for Meshwing...

Talen looked up at the skittery servo-sprite. Actually, while Meshwing wouldn't be able to fly the *Heart*, she understood how it worked.

'Can you help me send a distress call?' he asked the small robot.

The automaton replied with a series of excited bleeps. There was a buzz from behind and Talen swivelled around to see a host of the flying machines hovering behind them, their wire-framed wings humming. Of course. Fleapit and Mekki had been making a small army of the things! Perhaps he wasn't as alone as he'd originally thought.

He leant forward, Meshwing dipping down to listen to his instructions. 'We need to make sure the Necrons don't pick up the signal. Can you disguise it somehow?'

Meshwing trilled what Talen hoped was agreement and the servo-sprites went to work, flitting back and forth as they adjusted equipment and reprogrammed cogitators. Talen had no idea what they were doing, but trusted Mekki and Fleapit's genius. If they'd created the servo-sprites, the tiny robots would know what they were doing. At least, he hoped they did.

The flurry of activity stopped and the sprites hovered expectantly around Talen.

He shrugged at them. 'So, what do I do?'

Meshwing pointed at a big red button on the vox-console.

'I just press that?'

The servo-sprite nodded.

Talen flexed his fingers. 'If you say so.'

He pressed the button, and a faint pulse throbbed from the vox-casters. He glanced at the pict screen, expecting the Necrons to swoop down on the *Heart*'s communication array, but they continued flying back and forth, guiding the brainwashed refugees. Meshwing had done it! As far as Talen could tell, the call for help was being transmitted into the stars.

But how long would it take? Talen scratched the back of his hand nervously, tense seconds stretching into unbearable minutes. Talen felt his hope starting to fade. Who was he kidding? There was no way of knowing how far the transmission would travel, if there were any ships out there at all. Space was big and largely empty. Maybe he should try to fly the *Heart* out of here, after all. It couldn't be *that* difficult, could it?

His mind made up, Talen reached for the button, ready to kill the signal, when a voice burst from the speaker, the deepest voice Talen had ever heard.

'Unidentified voidship. We have intercepted your distress call. Please respond.'

'Transference? What do you mean, Transference? What does the Diadem really do?'

Zelia's question echoed around Merlek's throne chamber as she stepped forward, ignoring the dispassionate gaze of the assembled Necrons. She was shaking, her fists clenched and her eyes hard, staring up at the Necron Overlord and the mother he had stolen from her.

No sooner had Zelia spoken than Fleapit strode over to her, his usually loose movements strangely mechanical. She stood her ground, staring the mind-shackled Jokaero down. They could threaten her all they wanted. She'd been through too much to be silenced. She wanted answers.

'It is none of your concern,' the

Overlord boomed, still holding the Diadem before him.

'None of my concern? You blew up an entire planet, destroyed ships containing hundreds of people, killed my friend and enslaved my mum for that thing. I think the very least you owe me is an explanation!'

'I owe you nothing, human.'

Zelia took an involuntary step backwards as the Overlord descended the metal stairs leading from his throne, each footstep like a hammer striking an anvil.

'I am Merlek the Unconquered.'

Clank.

'I have commanded legions, vanquished entire worlds, and what are you?'

Clank.

'You are an insect.'

Clank.

'An insect.'

Zelia wanted to run. She wanted to cry and beg for forgiveness, but that was her fear talking. In the last few weeks, she had stood up to Tau and Orks. She had escaped death and disaster. She had crossed a galaxy to be here, and she wasn't about to go quietly.

'Yes, to you I am an insect, inferior in every way, but what does that make you, Merlek the Unconquered? Merlek the *bully* more like. You can threaten me all you like, but whatever you're planning it won't work. We'll stop you... and then what will they call you? Merlek the *hopeless*. Merlek the failure!'

'Silence!' The Overlord's bellow hurt Zelia's ears, but not as much as the hand that grabbed her. Fleapit had shot out a long arm, his fingers digging into her arm. She tried not to cry out, but couldn't help but gasp in pain. The Jokaero was too strong.

Merlek stopped in front of her, his head cocking to the side as if fascinated by her agony. 'Does it hurt?'

'No,' Zelia lied, only to whimper

seconds later as Fleapit tightened his grip. 'Yes…'

'And yet still you resist.' The Overlord seemed almost wistful. 'You are scared. You are in pain.' He looked around at his army, at the disintegrators in their hands. 'You are in mortal danger, and yet you dare defy me. A human child.'

There was no venom in the Necron's words. No anger. Only… fascination.

'You're curious.' Zelia turned at Mekki's voice, wincing as her arm twisted in Fleapit's grip. The Martian was peering at the Overlord, his electoos flashing.

'Do not presume to know me, Martian,' Merlek sneered, but Mekki ignored the obvious threat in the Necron's voice.

'You have felt pain. The pain of your consciousness being stripped out of your body, encased in necrodermis. Long, long ago. Before the Imperium. Before war.'

'There was always war,' the Overlord hissed.

'But not always the Necrons.'

Zelia felt Fleapit's grip loosen, just for a second. She looked at the Jokaero, seeing a glimmer of confusion on the alien's face, and realised what Mekki was doing. Back when they had been first stalked by the Necron Hunter, Mekki had connected his mind to Fleapit's implants, experiencing the Jokaero's memories first-hand. Now he was doing the same, but there were other memories in the mix. Fleapit had been linked into the Necrons' memory engrams. Was Mekki seeing the Overlord's past?

'Silence!' Merlek thundered, and Mekki cried out, clutching his head and collapsing to the floor. Fleapit let out a grunt, his fingers releasing just enough for Zelia to yank her arm free and run to the Martian, who was lying worryingly still. She gathered him in her arms, whispering his name, fearing the worst. His face was ashen, even by Martian standards, his lips bloodless and his flesh cold. Then he groaned softly, his eyes flickering open. Zelia broke into a worried smile, her tears splashing down onto Mekki's cheek.

'Oh, thank the Throne. I thought... I thought you were dead.'

'No...' said Mekki. 'But they might as well be.'

She frowned. 'What does that mean?'

'Living metal,' he wheezed. 'Trapped souls.'

A snort from behind snapped her head around. Fleapit was looming over them, nostrils flared, eyes glowing. Whatever connection Mekki had established was lost. The Necrons were back in control.

'You demand an explanation,' the Overlord hissed, 'and Merlek the *Merciful* will provide one, with a demonstration!'

A shout rang out from behind the Necron guards. The foot-soldiers parted so another of their number could stalk into the chamber, dragging a very familiar woman.

'Let go of me!' Amity snarled, trying to break free of the Necron's clutches. Her weapons were gone, and a dark bruise had blossomed across the side of her face, her left eye swollen shut.

'Zelia! Mekki!' she called out when she saw the children huddled on the floor, before turning her ire back on the Necrons. 'What have you done to them, you *monsters?*'

The Necron warrior threw the captain at its Overlord's feet. Amity tried to push herself up, swaying on her feet in front of Merlek. She looked from the Overlord to Elise Lor, who had joined her master.

'Let me guess. You snared her with one of those mind-control bugs.' She glanced at the Diadem in Merlek's hand. 'Well, you've got your precious tiara. Why don't you let us all go?'

The Overlord glared at her. 'Because we have great plans, rogue trader. Plans that begin with you.'

The Overlord released his grip on the Diadem, but the steel crown didn't fall to the ground. Instead it hung in the air, spinning on its axis, before, with the sound of a sword being drawn from a scabbard, it separated into two rings. One slid through the air towards Amity, while the other flew towards Merlek to settle on his headdress. All the time, Amity fought against her captors, twisting this way and that so her half of the Diadem couldn't slip over her head. It was a fight she'd never win.

Around the walls, the assembled

Necron warriors moved as one, their disintegrators swinging around to rest on Zelia and Mekki.

'Resist and your young friends will be atomised,' Merlek growled.

Amity glanced back over her shoulder, her one good eye full of concern, but the distraction was enough. The Diadem dropped down and shrank to fit around her head.

'At last,' Merlek exalted as both halves blazed with emerald light and Amity started to scream.

On the *Heart*'s bridge, Talen was starting to lose his temper. He had explained the situation over and over and yet the gruff voice was still barking questions over the vox. What was the current situation? How near was the Necron Monolith? Where was the Diadem?

'I've told you everything I know,' Talen pleaded, 'but I still don't know who you are! Can you help me? Can you help my friends?'

He waited, but there was no reply. The vox-button clicked as he pressed it again.

'Hello? Are you there? Can you hear me?'

The voice finally responded. *'Stand by.'*

Stand by? Stand by for what?

The answer came with the sound of an explosion and a rumble that shook the deck-plates beneath Talen's feet. That had come from outside.

He tried the picters but the screens displayed only static.

There was another impact, louder than the last. And another. And another.

Then there was gunfire, and the screech of Necron beamers. There was a battle raging outside and Talen couldn't see a thing! Perhaps the explosions had knocked out the cameras, but even as Meshwing and her duplicates went to work fixing them, Talen knew he couldn't wait.

He raced to the boarding hatch, lowering the ramp, and rushed outside, clamping his hands over his ears to block out the rattle of boltguns. Smoke hung in the air, reeking of scorched ozone, and Tomb Blades lay burning next to the ships the Necrons had brought down. Many of the Necrons themselves were sprawled on the ground, their bodies already regenerating.

Pastoria shook, as a teardrop-shaped drop pod landed nearby. It wasn't explosions that Talen had heard – it was help arriving from the stars.

Drop pods were blazing from above like meteorites, joining the others that had already landed, their battle-scarred sides peeling open to reveal the help the refugees so desperately needed.

Now Talen knew who had answered his distress call. He could see them slicing through the Necron lines, shooting down jetbikes and reducing the skeletal warriors to junk metal.

They were unstoppable, their bulky blue power armour bigger than an Ork, their weapons deadlier than a Tau battlesuit.

They were the defenders of humanity, the legendary *Adeptus Astartes*.

They were Space Marines!

CHAPTER THIRTEEN

The Great Experiment

Zelia didn't know what was worse, Amity's screams or the look of rapture on her mother's face. Merlek couldn't smile, his skeletal features set impassive and unmovable, but whatever emotions the Overlord was experiencing were playing out on the face of his human puppet. Even Fleapit's glowing eyes were wide, reflecting the emerald energy that crackled between the two halves of the Diadem.

Merlek stood, arms outstretched, his metal body pulsating. As Zelia watched in horror, the Necrons released Amity, stepping back as the rogue trader mirrored the Overlord's stance, her hands stretched out beside her, the fingers of her right hand even curled around an invisible staff.

Back on Aparitus, Inquisitor Jeremias had attempted to use the Diadem to transfer his corrupted consciousness into Talen's body. The procedure had failed, the inquisitor unable to operate the Necron artefact, but Merlek knew exactly how it worked. For all they knew the Overlord had built the device. Necrons hibernated all over the galaxy in vast tombs, waiting to arise and claim a universe they believed was theirs by right of conquest. There was no way of knowing how long Merlek had waited to put his plan into action.

But why? Why project his mind into Amity's body?

'Yesss,' the Overlord hissed. 'I can feel your pain, rogue trader. I can feel your body ache and the sweat cool upon your brow. It is exquisite!'

Zelia's mouth dropped open as

realisation dawned. She stood, risking a step forward. 'I know what you want,' she shouted over the sound of the transfer.

Merlek's head snapped around to her, Amity once again mirroring the movement. 'You know nothing.'

'Living metal and trapped souls – that's what Mekki said when he touched your memories. When he saw you for what you are.'

'No human can understand the Necrons.'

'And no Necron can understand humans. I'm right aren't I? You used to be like us once.'

'We are nothing like you.'

'Maybe not exactly, but I'm willing to bet you were flesh and blood. I don't know why you transferred your minds into these metal bodies of yours, but I bet that when it happened you lost more than you gained. Yes, you're immortal, but you can't feel anything. You can't feel the heat of a sun against your skin. The embrace of a friend.'

'These things mean nothing to us.'

'I don't believe you,' Zelia said, shaking her head. 'You want to know what it's like to be human. To feel what we feel.' She jabbed a finger at the Diadem. 'Why else would you build that thing?'

Behind her, Mekki muttered beneath his breath, his words confused, half-remembered from his contact with Fleapit and the scarab. 'Crypteks... commanded to build a prototype... a means to reverse bio-transference. To return Necrontyr minds to physical bodies.'

'I *am* right,' Zelia yelled triumphantly. 'But there must be a different way.' She threw her arms wide, turning on her heel to take in the entirety of the vast chamber. 'You have all this power. All this technology. Why not grow new bodies in vats, the way humans grow servitors or replacement limbs?'

'Why should I,' Merlek snarled, 'when

you have already grown our bodies for us? This is my will. We shall prosper. We shall grow. We shall be alive.'

The Overlord brought his staff down on the floor on the last word, the crack echoed by the Necrons in the chamber each stamping a metal foot in agreement. Zelia looked around at their blank faces, emotionless and yet somehow expectant. They were mad, all of them. An eternity buried in their tombs had driven them insane. But she wouldn't let it happen. She would stop them, once and for all.

Zelia burst forwards, running for Amity before Fleapit could stop her. She leapt for the Diadem, reaching to yank it from the rogue trader's head, only for metal fingers to snatch the back of her jacket. The Hunter flung her across the chamber. She thudded and skidded, the polished metal burning her cheek. When she looked up, both Merlek and Amity were glaring at her, and despite the fear she could see in Amity's eyes, the captain was mouthing the Overlord's words.

'The experiment is a success. Once the Transference is complete, my Necrons will transfer their minds into every last one of you!'

CHAPTER FOURTEEN

Stormravens

Merlek and Amity threw back their heads, tears of frustration rolling down the rogue trader's face.

'The moment is upon us,' they exalted. 'The Necrontyr reborn.'

The Necrons stamped in agreement, but the sound was drowned out by the explosion that reverberated through the pyramid, the chamber shaking with such ferocity that even the Necrons struggled to stay on their feet.

'What is happening?' the Overlord and Amity demanded as the Monolith shuddered beneath a fresh onslaught. Hololithic screens appeared in the air above them, showing the skies outside the pyramid, fire blossoming along the Monolith's slanted walls. The Necron battle station was under attack, armoured gunships emptying plasma cannons and guided missiles into the pyramid's defences. Zelia stopped herself cheering as one of the heavy Necron cannons was blown to pieces, taking with it a large chunk of the surrounding wall. The breach immediately began to seal, the necrodermis hull knitting back together automatically, but the Necrons had lost their advantage. Suddenly they weren't the most powerful beings on the planet.

Zelia had seen similar aircraft on Targian, engaging Necron Doom Scythes in the burning sky. The same hooked wings. The same ceramite plating.

Targian had fallen, but Pastoria still had a chance.

Talen had cheered when the Stormraven gunships had attacked the pyramid, but his enthusiasm had been dampened when legions of Tomb Blades had streamed from the Monolith in response.

Now the Space Marines seemed overwhelmed, no matter how many drop pods fell from the sky. The Necrons were everywhere, swooping down from above on their jetbikes or teleporting onto the ground. Soon the Space Marines were outnumbered, but they still fought on, advancing on the Necrons, who had formed a protective ring around the entranced settlers.

Talen, for his part, was feeling next to useless. Yes, he'd had the presence of mind to grab one of Amity's beamers when he ran from the *Zealot's Heart*, but he doubted it would do any good against a Necron foot-soldier. All he could do was hunker down behind the *Heart*'s boarding ramp and hope no one noticed him.

He had never felt so pathetic, especially when streams of burning energy cracked from the pyramid like a whip. They sliced through gunships and drop pods, making short work of even the Space Marines' battle-hardened power armour.

A Stormraven drove into the ground not far from the *Heart*. Talen peered through the smoke, realising it was only half the gunship that had crashed, the fuselage having been cleaved in two. But there was no mistaking the cry of pain from the twisted wreck. Perhaps he could do something after all. Talen put his fingers into his mouth and whistled. Meshwing and the servo-sprites swarmed out of the ship just as they had the time he'd tried to break into the *Scriptor* back on Targian.

This time they wouldn't attack – well, not him at least.

He broke cover and raced to the smoking gunship, the flying robots forming a shield around him, electro-probes at the ready. The Stormraven's cockpit was a mess, the canopy shattered and the frame twisted. Talen heaved on the buckled ceramite, the servo-sprites joined in, and inch by painful inch the canopy lifted, falling away as soon as gravity took over.

An Ultramarine lay in the pilot's seat, his legs trapped beneath crushed controls. A battered helm swivelled up to face Talen, a single bloodshot eye exposed through a smashed visor.

'Get out of here,' the giant growled, waving his would-be rescuers away with a hand the size of Talen's head. The ganger recognised the voice at once.

'You talked to me over the vox,' he said, swinging down into the cockpit and trying to lift the controls.

'It was your signal?' the Space Marine asked. 'You are Talen?'

'And you're well and truly trapped,' he replied, giving up. If a genetically engineered Space Marine couldn't pull free, Talen didn't stand a chance... but maybe someone else did.

'Meshwing,' Talen said, looking up at

the servo-sprite, 'can you cut him out?'

The sprite didn't answer. She didn't need to. Instead she went to work with her sisters, electro-probes sliding back into their fingers to be replaced by tiny welding lasers. Soon smoke was curling up as they disassembled the wrecked control panels piece by piece.

'What are those things?' asked the Space Marine.

'They were made by my friends,' Talen replied proudly. 'We were lucky you heard our signal.'

The Space Marine reached up, removing his dented helmet and flinging it aside. His broad face was streaked in soot, his head shaved smooth and his jaw chiselled to the point where it almost didn't look real. Luckily, he didn't seem to notice Talen staring.

'We were patrolling the area,' the Space Marine explained. 'My company has been searching for the Necron scum ever since Targian. We never dreamt there would be survivors.'

Talen frowned. 'Then why were you still looking?'

'To destroy the xenos,' the warrior replied, as if the answer were obvious.

'Well, I'm glad you're here,' Talen said as the sprites finished their work, the controls collapsing into their composite parts. 'Although the battle doesn't seem to be going well.'

The Space Marine pushed himself up to his full imposing height and surveyed the battlefield. His battle-brothers were being pushed back, the pyramid almost upon them. He growled as he saw gunships dissolve in the path of the particle whip.

'It is almost impossible to storm a Necron Monolith of that magnitude, even for Ultramarines.'

Talen scrambled up beside the monstrous warrior. 'I thought you could do anything?'

The Space Marine pointed at the throbbing crystal on top of the pyramid. 'We can, but a Necron Monolith has unlimited power and unbreakable defences.'

Talen considered this, turning to face his new ally. 'So far, so depressing – but what if you have people on the inside?'

CHAPTER FIFTEEN

An Honourable Sacrifice

Captain Fabian of the Ultramarines couldn't believe his genetically augmented eyes as Maccius ran up with a human boy and a swarm of what looked like robot-insects. Not that their sudden appearance stopped him from cleaving a Necron in two with his chainsword before emptying his boltgun into another.

'What are you doing, sergeant?' he snarled, surveying the field for more Necrons to put to the sword.

Maccius beckoned him behind a burnt-out voidship. If the captain had been surprised before he was completely incredulous by the time the sergeant had completed his report.

'You are suggesting we ally with *children*.'

'At least two of this boy's compatriots are on board the Monolith, brother-captain. They can assist us from within.'

A Tomb Blade swept overhead. Fabian downed the jetbike with a swift shot to its anti-grav generator. 'Children have no value as allies.'

Incredibly, the human boy seemed to take offence at this, thumbing his chest. 'If it wasn't for *this* child you would never have found the Necrons.'

Fabian reappraised the youth, who was scrawny but looked as though he could handle himself in a fight. 'You sent the distress signal?'

The boy nodded, and Fabian looked away long enough to blast the Necron pilot who was trying to untangle itself from its wrecked flyer.

The captain shook his head. 'It is

our duty to protect the children of the Imperium, not thrust them into battle!'

'My friends are already up there,' the boy argued, jabbing a finger at the pyramid. 'And besides, we've been in more battles these last few weeks than most Imperial Guardsmen. We've survived Genestealers, Tau, zombies and greenskins, not to mention a Necron Hunter.'

Fabian glanced at his sergeant. 'Is this true?'

Maccius nodded. 'Apparently so, brother-captain.'

Beside them, the Necron was regenerating. Fabian and Maccius raised their bolters as one and peppered it with shots.

The boy, meanwhile, wasn't giving up. 'We can help you, captain.'

Fabian growled, still not happy with the suggestion, but Maccius seemed convinced. 'Was I not much older than Talen when I first joined the Chapter, captain? Were you? Besides...' The ghost of a smile played over the sergeant's scarred lips. 'I have a plan.'

The throne room convulsed as Ultramarines missiles raked the hull. This was Zelia's chance. She broke into a sprint, making for the arched doorway on the far side of the chamber, gambling that the Necrons were too busy trying to stay on their feet to notice her make a run for it.

But her escape bid did not go unnoticed. Fleapit's head snapped around, his green eyes glowing. Soon he was at her heels, ready to tackle her to the ground.

She just had to make it through the doorway, out into the corridor beyond. She put everything into the final push and threw herself out of the chamber.

The mind-shackled Jokaero followed, but didn't notice Mekki waiting for him behind the door. The Martian jumped on Fleapit's back, knocking his friend to the floor. Fleapit reared up, but Zelia doubled back, grabbing the Jokaero's impossibly strong arms, doing her best to pin them down. Their plan had worked – Mekki sneaking out when the Necrons were preoccupied with the Space Marines – but Fleapit was fighting back now they'd lost the element of surprise!

'I won't be able to hold him for long!' Zelia cried out, as the Jokaero bucked beneath them.

'It will not take long,' Mekki promised, finding the scarab on Fleapit's neck and jabbing his haptic connectors into a seam that bisected the back of the metal insect. The scarab squealed, and Mekki's electoos flashed emerald green as he attempted to connect to Fleapit through the Necron bug.

'Come on, Flegan-Pala,' Mekki growled through clenched teeth. 'Listen to me. Free yourself.'

The entire thing had been Mekki's idea. He believed he could break through the Necron conditioning by flooding Fleapit's mind with his own memories: escaping Scarface, taking on Madame Lightbringer, running from Nettle-Nekk. They had achieved so much together, and had become stronger than they'd ever been on their own. If anything could bring Fleapit back to them, it was this.

But it wasn't working. Fleapit was snarling, foam speckling his lips. He was lost, nothing more than a feral beast controlled by an intelligence that only lived to destroy.

'Please, Fleapit,' Zelia pleaded as he almost threw her clear. 'You know us. You've protected us, and we've protected you. We're a team. We're—'

She was about to say 'friends' when she lost the fight. Fleapit pushed himself up, throwing both of them aside as if they were toys. Zelia crashed to the floor, Mekki pulling her away as the crazed Jokaero stalked towards them. They backed against the wall, nowhere else to go. Instinctively, Zelia put a protective arm in front of Mekki as Fleapit raised his hands above his head, fists ready to smash down on them. His lips drew back and he struck... reaching behind his neck and ripping the scarab clear. He squeezed, crushing the wriggling insect between his fingers, and hurled the remains as far as he could.

Then he turned and, without hesitation, gathered both Zelia and Mekki into a hug. When he finally released them, there were tears in his eyes, not of sorrow, but of rage. Zelia touched his face, and for once the Jokaero didn't flinch, leaning into her palm, his expression telling her everything she needed to know. He had been enslaved for the final time.

'What do we do now?' Mekki asked, as Fleapit glanced back at the throne room. The Hunter was standing motionless, defending its leader.

'We need to hide before they realise Fleapit is free,' Zelia said, jumping up.

'And what then?'

'Then we find a way of saving mum and Captain Amity.'

She spun around at the sound of hurrying footsteps. More Necrons were running to protect Merlek, while others manned cannons to fight off the attacking gunships. Grabbing Mekki's arm, she ushered her friends into an alcove, hiding in the shadows until the warriors passed.

A vox beeped noisily as the Necrons rushed into the throne room. Zelia winced, expecting a barrage of disintegrator beams to rip them apart, but the firestorm never came. She looked to her sleeve, forgetting that her own communicator was in pieces somewhere in the bowels of the pyramid. Beside her, Mekki answered the call, clicking his wrist-screen.

'Zelia? Mekki?' said a familiar voice. *'Are you there?'*

'Talen!' Zelia said, pulling Mekki's arm towards her. 'We're on the pyramid.'

'I know – exactly where we need you to be.'

She frowned. 'We?'

Another voice came over the line. *'Zelia Lor – this is Sergeant Maccius of the Ultramarines Third Company.'*

Zelia glanced at Mekki. Talen had teamed up with Space Marines?

'We need you to find the Necrons' teleportarium. Can you do that?'

'Yes,' Mekki replied eagerly. 'They teleported us on board.'

'And you can find your way back to it?'

Mekki looked a little insulted at the sergeant's question. 'Of course I can.'

'Then get moving,' Talen urged them. *'We haven't got long!'*

Mekki had been true to his word. He found the teleportarium at the first attempt. The chamber was empty, the Necrons having more important matters to deal with. Mekki activated the vox, telling Maccius they had arrived.

Zelia watched as the Martian took to the controls, following instructions from a Techmarine on the surface. He powered up the teleporter, entering coordinates provided by Maccius. She couldn't help but feel a swell of pride in her chest. Mekki had never looked so confident, so in control, his hands darting over the console. When she looked at the terminal, she saw only a jumbled mess of alien buttons and glyphs, but for Mekki it all made sense, his electoos flashing as he processed everything he'd learnt about the

Necrons since coming on board to follow the sergeant's instructions. Back on the ice planet Zelia had felt frustrated when watching Mekki work, now she saw him for what he was — a genius.

'Are you ready?' Maccius asked over the vox.

'Yes,' came Mekki's reply. 'The teleportarium is set. Just waiting for the word.'

'The word is given.'

Mekki yanked a lever into place and, with a discordant shriek, something began to materialise on the pad in front of them. Zelia swallowed, expecting to see Talen alongside a squadron of towering armoured giants, but the shape that formed on the platform wasn't Talen, and it certainly wasn't an Ultramarine.

It was a huge, ugly bomb.

'You're going to blow us up?' Zelia spluttered into the vox.

'The explosion should be enough to take out the Monolith from within,'

Maccius said, *'while we handle the Necrons on the ground.'*

Talen's voice came over the vox. *'But what about my friends?'*

Maccius's response was simple. *'They must teleport themselves to safety before the melta bomb detonates.'*

'No,' Zelia said sharply.

Mekki and Fleapit stared at her in shock.

'This isn't open to discussion,' Maccius told her.

'Neither is abandoning my mum,' Zelia replied. 'Or Amity for that matter.'

'Your mother is controlled by the Necrons,' Mekki pointed out sadly. 'And as for Captain Harleen Amity–'

'How long until detonation?' Zelia asked, cutting over him.

'Five minutes,' came the stern reply.

'Then we're going to have to move quickly,' she said, turning to her friends. 'Look – you two can teleport off the Monolith, but I'm getting mum.'

Mekki didn't even hesitate. 'Then we

are coming with you, Zelia Lor,' he said, and Fleapit nodded in agreement. 'We all leave together.'

CHAPTER SIXTEEN

The Final Battle

'What if they don't get off the pyramid in time?' Talen asked, as the vox went dead.

Maccius looked up from where they had been sheltering behind a Rhino battle tank.

'Then their noble sacrifice will be honoured.'

The Space Marine checked his bolter and nodded sharply towards the Techmarine and Captain Fabian.

'That's it?' Talen said, looking at each of them in turn. 'They help you sneak a bomb on board the Necron base and then... *boom?*'

'You will wait here,' Captain Fabian instructed him before leading his battle-brothers back into the fray.

Yeah, you really don't know me at all, Talen thought as soon as they were gone. Peeking around the tank, he saw the *Zealot's Heart* on the other side of the battlefield. It would be a dangerous run, but he could make it, especially with Meshwing's help. He whistled and the servo-sprites swarmed down from their perch atop the Rhino tank, once again forming a protective shield around him.

Blowing out to steady his nerves, Talen ran, ducking as an explosion blossomed nearby, grit and dirt raining down all around. That had been close – but not as close as a second explosion that saw him sprawling in the mud. His ears ringing, he tried to get up, but slipped, slapping back down to the ground. Tiny fingers grabbed his jacket, his belt, even his boots. Suddenly he was zipping across the battleground, flying inches from the floor. He craned his neck, seeing Meshwing at his shoulder. The servo-sprites were carrying him, their buzzing wings straining against the extra weight. Talen laughed, despite the danger, whooping as they swept up the ramp and deposited him in a heap in the *Heart*'s empty hold. He ran to the bridge, where the screens were now showing the fight outside: Ultramarines going toe to toe with Necrons as the pyramid continued its deadly salvo, frying Space Marines in their own armour.

A shadow fell across him and he realised that Grunt had lumbered to his side. The servitor was staring at the screens, the light from the explosions reflecting in his blank eyes.

'I wish the others were here,' Talen said to him, not expecting an answer. But he got one all the same. The servitor lived up to his nickname, grunting as he pointed towards the pilot's seat.

'Amity?' Talen asked. 'Yeah, her too. She'd know what to do, but I don't even know where she is.'

'Boop,' the servitor said.

Talen screwed up his face. 'What?'

'Boop,' Grunt repeated.

Talen's eyes went wide as he realised what the servitor was trying to say.

'Her homing signal.' He turned excitedly to Meshwing. 'Back on Hinterland Outpost, Grunt found Amity by tracking a homing signal on her jacket. Can you locate the signal?'

The servo-sprite flitted over to Grunt's head, connecting one of her probes into his cranial implant before flying back to the main terminal. The other servo-sprites joined her, pressing buttons and activating switches. Talen let them work until a steady beeping filled the bridge, repeating over and over.

'Boop,' Grunt said.

'Boop,' Talen agreed happily. 'That must be it, but where is it coming from?'

Meshwing activated the holo-projectors

and an image of the Necron pyramid appeared in the middle of the bridge, a flashing light near its peak.

'Is that her?' Talen asked, and Meshwing nodded. Talen blew out and rubbed his neck. Okay, they knew where Amity was. Now they just had to get her out...

'Transference must be completed,' Merlek commanded as the battle raged outside the Monolith.

From the doorway, Zelia and the others watched as the Overlord stared into Amity's eyes – eyes that would soon be Merlek's!

'Now what do we do?' Mekki asked after he'd finished counting the sheer number of Necron guards in the throne room.

Zelia's attention was fixed on her mother. 'We take a leaf out of Talen's book.'

Mekki looked at her quizzically and she smiled.

'Do you remember how he fooled Corlak on Aparitus?'

A grin spread over Fleapit's face.

Seconds later, Fleapit was dragging both Zelia and Mekki before the throne. They thrashed and struggled, but he would not let them go.

'The children have been recovered,' Elise proclaimed, but not everyone was convinced. The Hunter peered at them, its single eye pulsating, before delivering its verdict.

'No. The Jokaero is unshackled. It is a ploy!'

'Well, it was nice while it lasted,' Zelia yelled as the Hunter raised its gun. Fleapit released his grip, and Zelia rolled free, bringing up her digi-webber and firing globs of spider-silk at the Necron assassin. They found their target as it pulled the trigger, covering the Hunter's eye and chest. Its aim went wide and instead of atomising the children, the blast piled into Merlek, taking half the Overlord's metal body with it.

The Necron guards reacted immediately, turning their weapons on the traitor that had dared fire on their leader. They fired as one, the frenzy of disintegrator bolts ripping the Hunter's body apart.

'Now,' Zelia yelled, and Mekki activated his holo-bead. In an instant, they were surrounded by dozens of images from Mekki's recordings – roaring Ambulls and snarling Genestealers charging at the guards. The Martian had used the trick before to confuse their enemies, but never with the number of hololiths he created now. There were Tau, plague zombies and krakens, Orks, tech-adepts and Space Marines.

With the Necrons distracted, Zelia and Fleapit tackled Elise, pulling her down to the deck. She struggled and flailed, but this time Fleapit went to work on the scarab, his nimble fingers opening the silver bug and ripping circuitry from its central cogitator. The legs snapped back from Elise's neck and he yanked it clear, leaving red marks where it had attached itself to her nervous system. Elise blinked, her vision cleared, and she stared up into her daughter's face.

'Zelia? You're... you're here.' She glanced around herself. 'Actually, where *is* here?'

All around was confusion and danger, but Zelia didn't care. For one glorious minute, she ignored the sounds of battle and held her mum tight. Elise returned the hug, tears of happiness wet against Zelia's neck.

'You found me, my clever girl. You found me.'

'We have to go,' Mekki shouted, breaking the moment as he checked his wrist-screen. 'The bomb is due to—'

It was too late. Zelia felt the explosion before she heard it, blossoming deep below in the teleportarium. The floor lurched as the Monolith's anti-gravity generator failed. They were going to crash.

Beside them, what was left of Merlek's body ranted as it slid away, scrabbling with its one remaining hand. Its claws dug into the burnished deck, stopping it from falling, and it glared at the children who were holding on to the edge of the steps.

'I shall destroy you. I shall destroy you all.'

'No,' came a voice from behind. 'You will not.'

Zelia looked up, to see Amity struggling to stay on her feet. The captain reached up and pulled the Diadem from her head.

'You want this thing?' she spat. 'You can have it!'

Amity flung the crown like a discus. It swept over their heads, striking Merlek in the face. The Overlord lost his grip on the floor and slid down to his doom into the fiery mess of the teleportarium as the pyramid struck the ground.

Flames blossomed beneath them, the floor a sloping wall. Amity slipped, sliding down before Zelia reached out and grabbed her. The five of them clung onto Fleapit, who in turn clamped his fingers around the edge of a bent deck-plate, but it was no good. The throne room was collapsing around them, the walls buckling, the ceiling tumbling down.

'I'm sorry, mum,' Zelia yelled, burying her head into Elise's chest as she waited for the inevitable.

CHAPTER SEVENTEEN

Roots

'Now!'

Talen spun around from the controls as the *Heart*'s teleporter fired into life. Outside, the pyramid had been consumed in a fireball, the resulting shockwave almost knocking the voidship from its landing rig, but Talen didn't care. He was staring at the storm of impossible energy in front of him, willing his plan to work.

Talen jumped back as flames swept out from the teleporter, the cacophony of warped space finally collapsing in on itself to reveal a huddle of bodies clutched together on the pad.

'Yes!' Talen yelled, punching the air, as Zelia looked up from her mother's embrace. One by one, the survivors scrambled up, blinking as they glanced around in amazement, hardly believing they were still alive. Zelia raced forwards and flung her arms around him, joined seconds later by Mekki and even Fleapit. Talen laughed as he was nearly knocked from his feet. Only Elise and Amity remained on the teleporter, the rogue trader brushing soot from her sleeve.

'Not bad, kid,' she said, nodding at Talen. 'Not bad at all.'

The fires caused by the Monolith's destruction raged for days. The Space Marines rounded up and destroyed the remaining Necrons, who, without Merlek, lost their sense of purpose. Some simply dissolved into the air, while others were ground beneath the Ultramarines' boots.

As for the Diadem, it was nowhere to

be found. Captain Fabian's Techmarine concluded that it had been consumed in the pyramid's pyre, along with its Overlord.

The settlers, free of Merlek's control, decided to stay on Pastoria. The planet was no longer a secret but, as Maccius suggested, could serve the Imperium as an agri world.

Of course, such a venture would require farm equipment, and lots of it. Thankfully, Targ Outpost had a willing mechanic on hand.

'Are you sure you want to stay?' Talen asked Mekki as Amity readied the *Zealot's Heart* for take-off.

The Martian nodded, glancing back at the settlers, who were already rebuilding their habs. 'Yes, Talen. I can make a difference here.'

Talen laughed. 'Just Talen?' he replied. 'Not Talen Stormweaver?'

Mekki raised a quizzical eyebrow. 'Of course. We are friends, are we not? I see no need to be formal.' The Martian turned as Fleapit lolloped over to them. 'Besides, I shall have Flegan-Pala to help me.'

Mekki's expression faltered as the Jokaero shook his hairy head, clicking and snorting in response.

'What did he say?' Talen asked.

'That Pastoria only has room for one genius,' Mekki said, his voice catching, 'and he has plenty to get on with on board the *Heart*.'

'You're coming with us then, monkey-breath?' Talen asked, as the Jokaero bounded up the ramp towards a waiting Captain Amity.

'He's coming with *me*,' the rogue trader corrected. 'And my new co-pilot. Are you ready?'

Talen grinned, but held up a finger. He looked around, spotting Zelia beside the *Scriptor*, which had been recovered and brought back to camp. The planet-hopper had crashed when Zelia and the others were teleported away, and while damaged, would soon be space-worthy again.

Talen walked over to where Zelia was fixing the landing rig. He stopped, hesitating for a moment. He wasn't looking forward to this.

'So...' he stammered. 'We're, er...'

Zelia turned and smiled at him sadly. 'You're ready to go.'

Talen nodded. 'Amity says she's heard about a job on the Eastern Fringe. She hasn't technically got a Warrant of Trade—'

'But she has a crew.'

Talen glanced at the ground before meeting her gaze again. 'Yeah. Yeah, she has.'

Zelia sprang forward and held him tight. 'Look after each other.'

He returned the hug, not wanting to let go. 'We will.' Sniffing, he pulled himself free. 'And what about you?' He glanced up at the *Scriptor*. 'You nearly ready to fly?'

This time Zelia's smile didn't quite reach her eyes. 'Yeah. All systems go.'

'Glad to hear it,' Talen said as the *Heart*'s engines sounded. 'I better go.'

He started running towards the voidship, before turning to shout back at her. 'But if you're ever in the area, I'm sure we'll be bringing the *Heart* back this way from time to time...'

'I'll see what we can do,' Zelia called after him, waving as he turned and ran up the boarding ramp. Mekki joined her as she watched the hatch close, busying himself with Meshwing so Zelia couldn't see the tears in his own eyes. They were still watching when the *Zealot's Heart* rose into the air and blasted up towards the stars.

'That'll be us soon,' Elise said, walking up behind Zelia as she stared into the blue sky.

'Does it have to be?' Zelia asked.

Her mother looked at her, puzzled. 'What do you mean?'

Zelia turned, plucking up the courage to say what had been on her mind for days.

'We've spent our entire lives zipping from dig to dig, planet to planet.'

Elise grinned. 'That's the job, kiddo.'

'But does it have to be? Couldn't we stay, just this once?'

'Stay?' Elise repeated. 'Here on Pastoria?'

Zelia looked around herself, at the fields of swaying grass, at the settlers rebuilding their shelters. At Elise, Mekki and the servo-sprite.

'Why not?' she said. 'I'm fed up of always looking at the past, mum.'

'You want to make a future.' Elise smiled, putting an arm around her daughter and pulling her close. 'Then, that's what we'll do. We'll stay in one place. Put down some roots instead of digging stuff up.' She nodded. 'It'll be an adventure.'

Zelia grinned, happier than she had been for a long time.

She was home.

GALACTIC COMPENDIUM
PART SIX

ULTRAMARINES

Possibly the most famous of all the Space Marine Chapters, the Ultramarines have served the Imperium for over 10,000 years. Fierce warriors, the 'Sons of Guilliman' govern a sector of space in the Eastern Fringe known as Ultramar, marching into battle bellowing their war cry: 'Courage and honour!'

Like all Space Marines they are rarely far from their weapons, including the fearsome chainsword, with its whirring blades, and the bolter, one of the most powerful guns in the galaxy.

> ### DID YOU KNOW?
> By Imperial reckoning, there are approximately one thousand Adeptus Astartes Chapters, each containing one thousand Space Marines. That's a million superpowered soldiers protecting the galaxy from alien attack!

SPACE MARINE VEHICLES

Drop Pods – Fired into the heart of a battle from high orbit, drop pods travel at incredible speeds before smashing into the ground. Their ramps open on impact, delivering ten Space Marines at a time.

Stormravens – Armoured gunships capable of being fitted with twin-linked heavy bolters, Stormstrike missiles and lascannons.

Rhinos – A heavily armoured troop carrier and battle tank capable of withstanding direct hits from enemy fire, the Rhino can handle just about any alien terrain thanks to its rugged tracks.

TECHMARINES

Chosen from the ranks of a Space Marine Chapter for their natural affinity with machines, potential Techmarines are sent to Mars to train and hone their skills. They return with vastly expanded knowledge and their battle armour modified to include various servo-arms bristling with the tools needed to repair weapons and vehicles on the battlefield. Techmarines can instinctively feel any damage sustained by a piece of technology and commune with the 'machine-spirit' within a vehicle to help put things right.

NECRONS

Most people in the Imperium have no idea that the Necrons exist, let alone that they used to be flesh and blood. Once, they were the Necrontyr, beings who served a legendary race of Star Lords known as the C'tan. Long ago, they transferred their minds into bodies of living metal, achieving immortality but losing most of their memories. They have slept in vast tombs beneath the surface of countless worlds for generations, waiting to arise and claim a universe they believe is theirs by right.

Not all Necrons embrace their new existence, however. Some – such as the Ketatrix Dynasty – long to regain their senses of touch, taste and smell. These are the most dangerous Necrons of all, driven insane by their long sleep.

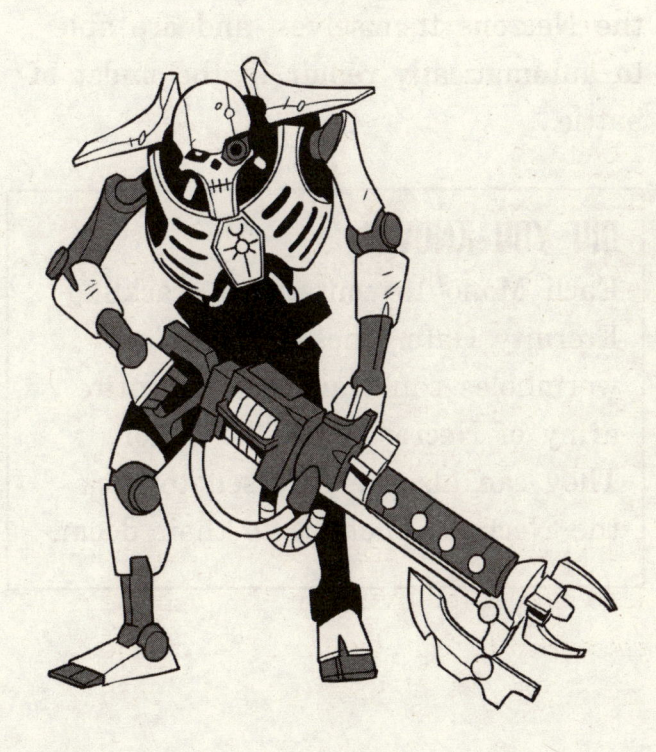

MONOLITHS

Necron Monoliths are huge, mobile pyramids that act as both floating fortresses and weapons of unbelievable destruction. Very little can breach the sloped sides of a Monolith, and they are armed with a terrifying particle whip. The pyramids are constructed from necrodermis, the same metal as the Necrons themselves, and are able to automatically repair in the midst of battle.

DID YOU KNOW?

Each Monolith contains a crackling Eternity Gate. These artificial wormholes can transport an entire army of Necrons into the action. They can also be reversed to suck the Necrons' enemies to their doom.

NECRON OVERLORDS

Most Necrons awaken as little more than mindless soldiers, functioning only to obey orders and enslave worlds. This isn't true of the Overlords, like Merlek, who retain most of their intelligence and cunning. These intimidating rulers command entire Necron Dynasties, with armies of foot-soldiers, weapons, fighters and vehicles under their control. They hover over battlefields in their Catacomb command barges, blasting enemies with bizarre and unstoppable weapons.

PSYKERS

A psyker is a being who possesses psychic powers. Most human psykers are rounded up and sent to Terra, where, if they can control their powers, they are permitted to serve the Emperor. Rogue psykers are hunted down by the Inquisition. Sanctioned psykers can also be found in the ranks of the Space Marines – these warriors are called Librarians.

> **DID YOU KNOW...**
> Astropaths are psykers who transmit messages across the vastness of space, far beyond the limitations of traditional vox-relays. All astropaths are blind, their eyesight lost through the realisation of their powers.

IMPERIAL FAUNA

The Imperium puts the *wild* into wildlife! Here are just some of the beasts you could come face to face with on your travels.

Chemdog – Native to the planet Vostroya, these savage canines are descendants of the original hounds brought by human settlers. Hundreds of years of radiation and chemical poisoning have mutated them into monsters.

Great Barking Toad – Found on Catachan, this noxious amphibian is considered the most poisonous creature in the known universe. If threatened, it emits a gas that can wipe out life for miles around.

Grox – Able to thrive anywhere, these large reptiles are now farmed throughout the Imperium, their meat consumed by soldiers and citizens alike. Unfortunately, farming grox is a dangerous pastime, as the savage beasts have a habit of attacking anything that moves, including other grox.

Phyrr-cat – A giant cat so stealthy that you could be standing right next to one and not know it's there – until it pounces!

Temple-weavers – Huge spiders that make their home in ancient ruins, they are notable for having ten legs instead of eight, and being the size of a battle tank.

TOMB BLADE

Vehicle type: Jetbike

Tracking devices: Nebuloscope

Pilot: Necron warrior

Weapons: Tesla Carbines, Particle Beamers, Shadowlooms

ELISE LOR

Zelia's mother, Elise Lor, is an explorer and archaeologist who specialises in the technology of long-lost civilisations. It is a dangerous profession. Not only are many of her dig-sites swarming with terrifying monsters, but the Imperium has also banned knowledge of much of the past, especially artificial intelligence.

Elise brought up Zelia alone after her husband was killed on a previous expedition. Mother and daughter have travelled the galaxy with Elise's assistant, Mekki, and fellow explorer Erasmus on their ramshackle planet-hopper, the *Scriptor*, which is piled high with souvenirs of their travels. The *Scriptor* is constantly in a state of organised chaos, but has been their only true home for many, many years.

THE ZEALOT'S HEART

Once the ship of inquisitor Jeremias Drayvan, this sleek black vessel was commandeered by rogue trader Harleen Amity after the destruction of her own ship, the *Profiteer*. As well as the latest vox-devices, the *Zealot's Heart* has a fully working teleporter, able to transport its crew to the surface of any planet, although the transfer isn't always a pleasant experience!

ABOUT THE AUTHOR

Cavan Scott has written for such popular franchises as *Star Wars, Doctor Who, Judge Dredd, LEGO DC Super Heroes, Penguins of Madagascar, Adventure Time* and many, many more. The writer of a number of novellas and short stories set within the *Warhammer 40,000* universe, including the *Warhammer Adventures: Warped Galaxies* series, Cavan became a UK number one bestseller with his 2016 World Book Day title, *Star Wars: Adventures in Wild Space – The Escape*. Find him online at www.cavanscott.com.

ABOUT THE ARTISTS

Cole Marchetti is an illustrator and concept artist from California. When he isn't sitting in front of the computer, he enjoys hiking and plein air painting. This is his first project working with Games Workshop.

Dan Boultwood is a comic book artist and illustrator from London. When he's not drawing, he collects old shellac records and dances around badly to them in between taking forever to paint his miniatures.